AN UNCERTAIN ACCOMPLICE

POISON TOE PRESS
2018

AN UNCERTAIN ACCOMPLICE

DONALD LEVIN

A MARTIN PREUSS MYSTERY

Inquiries should be addressed to
Poison Toe Press
PO Box 206
1221 Bowers
Birmingham, Michigan 48012

ISBN: 978-0-9972941-4-9

Cover by Publish Pros
www.publishpros.com

First edition published 2018
Printed in the United States of America

This book is for Suzanne Allen and Jerry van Rossum

One day you will do things for me that you hate. That is what it means to be a family.

—Jonathan Safran Foer,
Everything is Illuminated

Sunday, July 15, 2012

1

The call came while Martin Preuss sat on the group home's back patio on a steamy summer afternoon.

The house was air conditioned, but his son Toby loved being outdoors no matter the weather, so Preuss was braving the heat beside him. Toby began to fidget in his wheelchair, and Preuss was just about to take him inside to see if he needed to stretch out in bed when his cell phone rang.

He looked at the number and considered punching Ignore. But as the phone continued to ring, he decided he was more curious than annoyed and took the call.

"Martin," the woman's voice said at the other end of the line. "Hi! It's been *ages!*"

"Well," he said, "this is a surprise."

"How *are* you? It's so good to hear your voice," Shelley Larkin went on, without giving him a chance to reply.

"Listen," she said, "I have something you might be interested in. It's right up your alley, and I *have* to talk to you about it. Can we meet? Like, today?"

"Can't you tell me over the phone?"

"It's better if we talk in person. Besides, there's someone who wants to meet you. Are you in Ferndale? How soon can you meet me there?"

"I'm not home. I'm spending the day with my son."

"Bring him along."

"Things are a little crazy in Ferndale. The Pig and Whiskey street fair is on now. You know that, right?"

"I *do*," Shelley said. "That's *exactly* where I want to meet you."

An hour later, Preuss stood beside Toby in his wheelchair next to a giant inflated replica of a Jack Daniel's bottle, twenty feet high, in the middle of East Troy Street, which was blocked off to accommodate the street festival. Crowds jostled them without apology, and the more rambunctious bumped the wheelchair and continued on as if nothing happened.

Toby, of course, loved it . . . the crowds in constant motion, circling above and beside him with their tumult of laughter and loud voices, flashes of light and dark and color (all he could see with his limited vision, especially with sunglasses on), the pungent smells of barbecued pork and fried dough and alcoholic drinks served in tents lining both sides of the street, the distorted scream of the guitars in the Latin blues group on the bandstand down the block . . . what wasn't to love?

Toby gave out with a low foghorn scream that sailed up to a joyful falsetto. He raised his narrow shoulders and brought the backs of his hands together, his wrists severely bent from the contractures of his cerebral palsy. He rocked from side to side in his wheelchair, one happy guy.

"Yeah," Preuss said, leaning down to rub his son's shoulders, "this is your kind of thing. Me, not so much."

He straightened the Detroit Tigers cap on Toby's sweaty head and scanned the faces of the women who passed in the mostly male crowd. Preuss checked each pair of eyes for the downturned outer edges he remembered. Checked each pair of eyebrows for the silver chunks of studs. Checked each mouth opened wide in laughter and good times for that one crooked tooth he still thought about, the canine on the upper right overlaying the incisor ever so slightly, the imperfection a charming corrective to her pretty face.

But all he saw were tattoos and baseball caps worn backward and red Solo cups sloshing over with amber booze from the booths dispensing Jack Daniels, Maker's Mark, Tito's Vodka, Jim Beam, and all the other liquor.

Shelley Larkin materialized out of the crowd. Once, seeing her would have given him great pleasure, he reflected. Now she's just another young woman in a "Made in Detroit" tee shirt.

Right, he thought. Just keep telling yourself that.

Coming forward, she raised a slender hand in greeting. She smiled.

That tooth.

She had let her hair grow out in its natural texture and color. She no longer dyed it a deep black that let no light escape. It fell across her face in a relaxed, honey-colored wave that she brushed aside when she spotted him.

She was leading someone, another woman, younger than Shelley in a brown spaghetti-strap top advertising Bushmills with tan lettering inside the whiskey's Celtic knot logo. The woman hung back, and Shelley had to grab her by the arm and pull her along.

"Hi," Shelley said when she was close enough, showing her crooked tooth in a broad grin.

Maybe I'm not so over her as I thought, Preuss considered; I always was a sucker for that fang.

She wrapped him in a hug, and he momentarily held the frail bird bones of her shoulders.

She pulled back and said, "Martin Preuss, this is Jessie Douglas. Jessie, Martin's the guy I was telling you about."

The other woman nodded warily, no hand extended. She was in her mid-twenties, maybe five-six, with long, unkempt dark hair held back under a Bushmills cap, her face pale and waxen beneath aviator sunglasses. Her body was stout, and she wore frayed denim shorts cut high over thick thighs.

"Jessie," he said. He reached out a hand, which she shook. Her grip was loose, as though she were keeping herself ready to bolt from his grasp.

She looked at him with the same care he was examining her. "You're the private detective?"

"I am." He handed her one of his business cards. She glanced at it and stuffed it in her shorts pocket. She looked at Toby in his wheelchair beside Preuss. "Who's this?"

"My son, Toby."

"So *this* is Toby!" Shelley cried, and Toby gazed up at the source of his shouted name.

"He is," Preuss said, and realized she had never met his son. He had spoken of Toby to her (back when they talked regularly), and she had talked about wanting to meet him. But they never got that far.

"Toby," Preuss said, "this is Shelley."

Shelley reached for Toby's bent hand, and he reflexively pulled it away. She took it anyway and held it.

"I've heard so much about you," Shelley said, and laid a palm on the back of Toby's head. The boy gave her his flirtatious crooked grin. He turned his head and looked at her out of the corner of his eye, where his limited vision was best.

"Aren't you a handsome young fellow?" she said. Toby chirped happily.

"So," Preuss said, "what's up?"

"I was telling Jessie about you. Jessie," she said, turning back to the other woman, "you can trust this guy."

"Yeah?"

"Oh yeah. He's cool."

Jessie looked at Preuss again, as though testing that opinion. She buried her hands in her skimpy shorts pockets and looked at Shelley Larkin, waiting for her to take the next step.

"Go on," Shelley said. "Tell him."

Jessie didn't say anything, and Shelley said, "Martin, Jessie needs your help."

"Okay."

Jessie gave Preuss another once-over without speaking.

"Somebody want to tell me something?" Preuss said.

Shelley nudged her and Jessie stepped in closer. "It's my dad," she said finally.

"Okay."

"He died a couple weeks ago. In prison."

"Sorry to hear it."

"Yeah, thanks. Thing is, the crime he did, it wasn't totally his fault."

"Uh-huh."

Jessie caught the doubt in his voice and threw a sharp look at Shelley.

"Jessie," Preuss said, "most people in prison, you ask them, they'll say they're innocent."

"Okay, but, so, here's the thing. I talked to him the day before he died. He had cancer. He knew he was dying. He told me he did it, what he was charged with, which I always knew. But he said somebody put him up to it. And helped him do it."

"What was he in for?" Preuss asked.

"Felony murder."

"Pretty serious charge."

"I want somebody to look into this." Gone was the skittish doubt. Here was someone who craved something desperately. "I want to find out who put my father up to it, and I want them brought to justice."

"None of this came out at the trial?"

"I was just a little girl at the time, so I'm not exactly sure what came out. But I do know my father wasn't well back then. He had some serious mental issues."

"But he was competent enough to stand trial?"

"That's what they said. And he was the only one punished, I'm sure of that."

"How long ago was this?"

"He went to prison in '93."

"Did he say what he meant by 'somebody put him up to it'? He didn't mention a name?"

"I asked him, but he was in such bad shape at the end he couldn't concentrate very well. He was in terrible pain, he was all doped up with medication. So no, he didn't give me a name."

"Have you been to the police?"

She huffed impatiently. "They laughed me out of the station."

"Jessie," Preuss said, "is it possible your father's condition at the end affected what he told you?"

"Meaning what?"

"Meaning, if he was in such pain, maybe his thought process-es weren't quite right."

Jessie Douglas clucked her tongue, gave her head an angry shake, said, "Forget it." She turned away.

"Jessie," Shelley said, "wait."

"He's the same as the others," Jessie threw back over her shoulder. She disappeared into the crowd.

"I'm going after her," Shelley Larkin said.

"No," Preuss said. "Let her go."

"But I told her you could help her. She's just confused."

"How do you know her?"

"She called the *Voice* a couple weeks ago, said she wanted to talk to a reporter, tell her story and get some attention to her father's case. The editor sent her to me. I'm on staff there now," she added. "Full-time."

"Nice for you."

"Yeah. Good to have a little security."

When he met her, Shelley Larkin had been a stringer for the *Metro Voice*, a local alternative weekly.

"So you're doing an article on her?" Preuss asked.

"I'm not sure. Story might be kind of interesting, don't you think?"

"Not from what I've heard so far."

"Oh, I do. Miscarriage of justice-type thing? Readers love it."

"Sounds like her father did what he was convicted of. Where's the miscarriage?"

"That's what she wants to find out. Would you look into it? Just take a few hours, see if there's something there?"

"I don't think so." He looked into her face—that face he had seen in his mind's eye for so long. She laid a warm, moist hand on his arm. He felt put out, as though she were asking him to honor a history they had never shared.

"Please? She needs your help."

"What's this guy's name? Her father."

"Raymond Douglas."

"Wait," he said. "Her father is Ray Douglas?"

She nodded. "You know him?"

"Not personally," Preuss said, suddenly interested. "But I've certainly heard of him."

"Well," she said, "don't hold back. Do tell."

2

"I'd just started in uniform when it happened," Preuss said, "but it was a big deal around here. Ray Douglas was from Ferndale."

He picked up his iced tea and swirled the cubes around. To get out of the heat, they settled themselves at a table in the rear of Howe's Bayou, a low-lit Cajun restaurant on Woodward. Only a few tables were occupied; most of the action was at the street fair. The accordion windows in front were open to the traffic and hubbub of the main avenue, but Preuss and Shelley were sitting far enough in the back of the place to have a quiet space to talk.

In his wheelchair beside Preuss, Toby sat listing in a deep slumber; the hot weather and stimulation of the day's outing had been too much for him.

Preuss gently repositioned his son and said, "From what I remember, he was convicted of kidnapping and killing the wife of a local businessman. He was picked up pretty fast—I seem to remember his daughter was involved, too, somehow. That must have been Jessie."

Shelley took a sip of her beer and hid a small burp behind her fingers. "'Scuse me. She told me she's had a tough life. She didn't go into detail, but she implied she's just getting her shit together now."

He considered that. "This happened twenty years ago."

"Her story touched me. That's when I thought you might be able to help. I knew you were retired from the police, but I heard you were doing some private work."

"How'd you hear that?"

"I have my sources." She flashed a smile.

That tooth.

"Look," she said, "if you don't think there's anything here, that's fine. I just thought: Old crime, new angle, local connection." She shrugged. "Maybe I could still make a pitch to my editor. And if he wasn't interested, I'd go to *Hour Detroit* or some other outlet. Plus," she added, "it was a chance to connect with you again."

She took another sip of beer and her eyes crawled over the rim of her glass to fix him with an ironic gaze.

Okay, he thought. Now I'm being played.

Same old same old. He remembered how it had been a mistake to count on her sincerity; though she came across as all candor, she was a manipulator, with the habit of telling him what he wanted to hear. And she was remarkably good at doping that out.

She rested the glass on the table. "How've you been?"

"Same as ever."

"Seeing anyone?"

"Not really." Then, thinking about the trouble he had been having sorting things out with Janey Cahill, his former colleague in the Ferndale PD, he said, "Actually, it's complicated."

"Usually is."

Before he could reply, Toby awoke with a snort. He looked up, and a quick seizure gripped him. His arms and legs went straight out, his face twisted into a grimace.

Preuss stood and bent over his son, who was now trembling and whimpering. Preuss put his arms around the boy and murmured words of comfort. The only thing to do when these hit was to make sure he was safe.

In seconds, Toby's grimace turned into a smile, and his whimpering became a throaty chuckle.

"That one hit the funny button?" Preuss asked him.

Toby relaxed his arms and legs and coughed once. The signal his seizure was over.

"Is he okay?" Shelley asked.

"Now he is. The heat gives him seizures sometimes."

Preuss could smell Toby had evacuated his bowels during the episode.

"Look," he said, "my son needs his pants changed. And he's going to want to lie down after this. I have to go."

"No problem," she said. She gulped down the rest of her beer and stood. "So what's next? Will you take this on?"

"I could look into it. But only if she wants me to. Seemed like she didn't get the right vibes from me."

Shelley waved that away like so much smoke. "I'll talk to her, make her see your many fine qualities."

"Up to you." He unlocked the wheels on Toby's chair and eased him away from the table. "Talk to you later."

"I'll look forward to it," said Shelley Larkin.

The evening nurse pulled the sheet up to Toby's chin and patted his shoulder and left the room. The boy was stretched out on his bed in the group home. He worked his jaw like an old man and hummed softly to himself as he drifted into sleep. All the activity and heat of the day had worn him out.

Preuss reached over and turned out the lamp on Toby's night-stand. The light from the hallway gave the room a soft glow. On a CD, Judy Collins sang quietly about the salt of the earth.

As he relaxed from his own day, Preuss took his temperature about seeing Shelley Larkin. A few years before, they had tiptoed around a relationship—or he had tiptoed, more accurately. He thought they were moving toward something until she told him she was already seeing someone. The someone turned out to be another woman, who gave him the serious hairy eyeball the one time he had seen her.

Still, Shelley would text him to say hello occasionally. At first, he ignored them, then he started responding. When she would never reply, he stopped answering or even reading her texts. Before today, he hadn't heard from her for months.

And now, as usual, she got in touch with him because she wanted something from him.

He thought he had finally gotten her out of his system, but he had to admit seeing her gave him a small electric thrill.

He tried to put her out of his mind, and had just about succeeded when his phone rang.

He answered before it woke Toby.

"Is this Mr. Preuss?" A woman's voice.

"It is."

"It's Jessie Douglas. So I just got off the phone with Shelley Larkin. She said you're going to take the case?"

"Not exactly. What I said was, I'd look into it, but only if you wanted me to. If not . . ."

"No, no, I do. Look, I'm really sorry about today. I was way out of line."

"No worries."

"I don't know what came over me. I was so rude . . . I'm usually not like that. Few too many samples of the Bushmills, maybe."

She forced a dry chuckle and said, "Can we hit reset and try again? I might have found some useful information. Can we meet tomorrow?"

He thought about his schedule for the next day. He had a new client coming in at two to talk about a background check for new hires at her workplace; in the morning, he had to work on other projects.

"What are you doing for lunch?" he asked. "I've got some time around noon."

"Perfect. Name a place and I'll be there."

"There's a Noodles on Telegraph just north of Twelve Mile. Can you make that?"

"I'll be there."

"Great. See you then."

"So does this mean you'll do it?"

"We'll talk more tomorrow."

"The thing you have to realize is, my father was basically a good man."

Except for the part about murdering an innocent woman, Preuss thought. After first kidnapping her.

"He always loved me, no matter what."

Preuss said, "We'll talk tomorrow. We'll need to get some formalities out of the way before I can start."

"Like what?"

"Financial arrangements, for one thing. We ask for a retainer."

"How much?"

"For something like this, most likely fifteen-hundred."

"Can I put it on a credit card?"

"Sure."

"Great. Can I give you the number now?"

"Hang on," he said. "I don't deal with the money. Our office manager handles that. Her name's Rhonda Citron."

"Can I call her with it?"

"You can. Tomorrow."

"That's okay," Jessie said. "I'll take care of it. I want to get this going."

"Call if your plans change tomorrow, okay? Otherwise, I'll see you at noon."

"Will do. Thank you *so much*."

Preuss disconnected and remained seated in the chair beside Toby's bed. His face was stiff with fatigue. He rubbed feeling back into his cheeks, gave a massive yawn, but still couldn't muster the energy to stand up.

It was a little after nine o'clock. He closed his eyes for a moment to gather himself for the trip home.

He awoke to someone shaking his shoulder. The night aide stood over him with a look of concern.

"I didn't mean to disturb you," she said. "Nobody seems to know if you meant to spend the night or not."

"No," Preuss said. "I'm just relaxing before I take off. Is Toby okay?"

"He's fine." She gave him an odd smile. "The thing is, you've been asleep for hours. It's after one in the morning."

He blinked at her, groggy and dry-mouthed. "Seriously?"

"Seriously," she said, and leaned over to adjust Toby's head on his pillow. The boy snored quietly, gentle trills like little purrs.

Monday, July 16, 2012

3

Rhonda Citron sat straight-backed behind her desk in the reception area of the offices of Greene and Preuss, Investigations, in a low building on Telegraph north of Twelve Mile Road in Southfield. Thin, with a deathly-pale complexion and dressed all in black from head to toe despite the hot summer morning, she wore her long bleached blonde hair pinned up higher than usual in a complicated construction of curls and tendrils. Preuss wondered if an armature held up her towering do.

"Morning," she said pleasantly.

"Morning."

He had lain awake until five, and then, just as he decided to roll out of bed to start his day, he fell asleep. He woke with a headache too late to get over to Toby's to help get his son ready for his day program, so Preuss went straight into the office.

"Got a visitor," Rhonda said. She pointed the top of her hairdo toward the sofa at the side of the room, where Reg Trombley was unfolding his lanky frame and getting to his feet. Preuss's former colleague in the Detective Bureau in the Ferndale Police Department was tall and model-handsome with a long, fine-boned face and smooth caramel skin.

He was not, however, smiling as he usually was when he saw his friend and one-time mentor. Instead, Trombley brought his lips together grimly and reached out a hand. "My brother," he said.

They shook and folded each other into a hug. Trombley said, "Got a minute?"

"Sure," Preuss said. "Come in."

Rhonda said, "Either of you gents want coffee?"

Preuss looked to Trombley, who shook his head. Preuss said, "I'd love one, thanks," and led Trombley into his office.

When Preuss joined Manny Greene's private investigation firm the year before, after retiring from the Ferndale PD, Manny and Rhonda had converted a storeroom for his use as an office. Both Manny and Rhonda were compulsively neat, so when Preuss occupied the space, no boxes of stationery, office supplies, or old files were remaining. Preuss had no such tendencies. Out of respect for Manny and Rhonda, he tried to keep his desk cleaner than the one in his old office in the Detective Bureau, always piled high and deep with files and notes.

So when Trombley followed him into the office and closed the door behind him, there were no files or boxes to remove from the visitor's chair so Trombley could sit. Except for a photo on his desk of his late wife, Jeanette, his missing son, Jason, and Toby, he had not personalized the bare room in any way.

"This doesn't feel like a social call," Preuss said.

"No," Trombley said, "it isn't."

He reached into his pocket and removed his notebook. While he thumbed through to a page, Rhonda rapped on the door and entered with a mug of coffee. She placed it on Preuss's desk, and he nodded his thanks and she withdrew.

Trombley said, "Know a woman named Jessica Douglas?"

"I met her yesterday."

"When?"

Preuss blew across the lip of the mug and took a sip of steaming hot coffee. He had asked these same questions enough times to know where this conversation was headed. "I met her for the first and only time for five minutes late yesterday afternoon. At the Pig and Whiskey."

"That would be what time?"

"Quarter past four. What happened?"

"Her body was found early this morning."

Preuss sighed and sat back in his chair. "Where?"

"A crew came in to clean up from yesterday and found her in a dumpster. Alley behind Woodward, between Nine Mile and East Troy.

Trash tossed on top of her, like somebody was trying to hide her in a hurry. So you didn't know her well?"

"No," Preuss said, "I just met her the once. Then we talked again on the phone last night for a few minutes."

"What time?"

"Little after nine."

"What about?"

"We got off on the wrong foot when we met. She wanted to start over. She asked me to do a job for her. What brought you to me?"

"She had your card in her pocket."

Preuss nodded. "I gave her one when she waffled about going ahead."

"What was that about?"

Preuss thought for a moment. He had not formally agreed to take on the job, and it was moot anyway with the woman dead. He had no reason to keep information from his friend.

"Her father died in prison recently, and she wanted me to look into what she thought was some kind of conspiracy that got him locked up."

"What did you tell her?"

"We were supposed to meet again today and talk more about it. Then I'd let her know about taking it on or not."

Trombley scrawled in his notebook. "This on your own, or for the agency?"

"Agency. If we agreed to go forward, my plan was to do some spadework first, see what I could find out, then go from there."

"She got in touch with you, is that how you connected?"

"Remember that reporter from the *Metro Voice*, Shelley Larkin?"

"The one you were seeing?"

"'Seeing' is pushing it," Preuss said. He took another sip of coffee. "This was the first I'd heard from her in a while. Jessie was shopping around for a reporter to dig into the story, and she wound up with Shelley. Who reached out to me."

"And your contact with her didn't go beyond this one meeting?"

"And the phone call last night, correct."

Trombley thought about that. "Who was her father?"

"Guy named Raymond Douglas."

Trombley shook his head. "Dunno the name."

"It was a big thing twenty years ago. Way before your time. Went to prison for kidnapping and killing a woman. Right before he died, Jessie said he told her somebody put him up to it. She wanted to find who that was and bring them to justice."

"And that's what she wanted you for?"

"That's what she wanted *somebody* for. I was the closest she got to anybody saying yes."

Trombley wrote more in his notebook, then said, "She mention any other names?"

"No."

"Didn't say who her father was talking about?"

"No."

"How'd she seem? Upset? Worried about anything?"

"Nervous at first, but that seemed to be more about meeting me than anything else. Last night on the phone, she was just anxious to get started."

"Anything else you can tell me?"

Preuss shook his head. "How'd she die?"

"Strangled, by the looks of it. She had no purse or money on her. Could be a crime of opportunity."

"Or made to look like one."

"Could be," Trombley admitted. "And then they left her in a damn dumpster."

"Like just another piece of garbage."

"What people do to each other, man. Turns my stomach."

Trombley put his notebook away and got his feet under him to stand. "Do you have Shelley Larkin's numbers?"

"I do." Preuss pulled up her name (which he had recently put back into his iPhone after deleting it two years before) and read off the numbers for her cell and office.

"I'll check in with her," Trombley said, "see what she has to say. Meantime, call me if you hear anything?"

"Will do," Preuss said. "You'll keep me in the loop?"

"Much as I can," Trombley promised. "I would have called you down to the scene when I found your card, but the boss was there."

"He still looking over everybody's shoulder?"

"Not as bad as it was. He finds out you're involved, he'll be on me like white on rice, so I'm gonna keep that information to myself. They still don't much like you. Even after all this time."

"The feeling is entirely mutual."

They shook hands, hugged, and Trombley opened the door to Preuss's office and was gone.

Rhonda appeared in his doorway. "Before I forget," she said, and handed him a phone call slip. She had written *Jessie Douglas* on it, along with a phone number.

The name sent a cold shiver down his back. "When did this come in?"

"Last night. She left a message with the answering service. I picked it up when I got in. She gave a credit card number to pay for a retainer."

"I talked to her last night. I thought she was going to wait till this morning."

"So she's a new client? When can she come in to the sign the agreement?"

"She won't. She turned up dead this morning."

"Are you serious?"

"That's what Reg wanted to talk to me about."

"Oh my. So we should dispose of her credit card number?"

He thought for a few moments, then said, "First, see who the number belongs to. In fact, see what you can find out about her in general. We'll go from there."

"If she's dead, the case is, too, no?"

"Let's keep it open for a bit."

"But who's going to pay her bill?"

He thought about the young woman left in the garbage dumpster with the life squeezed out of her, soaked in whisky from rank plastic cups and buried in boxes reeking of rotting pork and greasy bones from the weekend's street fair.

"Let's not worry about that now," he said. "Do you still have those secret contacts of yours?"

"Sure."

He tore a sheet of paper from the pad on his desk and wrote a name on it. "Can you get me the trial transcripts for this guy?"

She took the paper and read out, "Raymond Douglas. What's his story?"

He gave her the short version of Douglas's story and she said, "No problem. He's related to Jessie Douglas?"

"Her father," Preuss said. "She asked me yesterday about doing a job for her connected to this guy's case."

"So you're going to be helping Detective Trombley with his investigation?"

"I'm sure Reggie wouldn't mind," Preuss said. "I'm also sure the chief of detectives would rather stick hot pins in his eyes than have me anywhere near this."

4

Shortly after noon, Rhonda handed him a CD. "All the documents for the Douglas trial," she said. "Trial transcripts, transcripts of the pre- and post-trial hearings, police interviews and interrogations, photos entered into evidence, all the key trial documents . . . the whole nine yards."

She had been a student in law school before a nervous breakdown caused her to withdraw and take time to get herself together, but she still maintained undisclosed contacts in the profession and could materialize surprising things on occasion.

"Rhonda, I've said this before, but I'll say it again. You are amazing."

She shrugged, gave him a wan smile. "It's what I do."

He closed himself in his office and began going through the disc. He refreshed his memory of the details. Raymond Douglas was convicted of entering the home of William and Claire Seldon and kidnapping Claire in 1992. The killer was a veteran of the first Iraq War who had applied for the position of police chief of Ferndale but had been turned down as having no qualifications for the job. Evidently, he hatched a plan to kill a prominent citizen, leave town for a while, and then return to solve the case by framing an innocent person. He would then (according to his plan) be rewarded with the police chief's position after all.

So one spring morning, Douglas dragged Mrs. Seldon from her home in Bloomfield Hills and put her in the trunk of his car. He drove her out to a deserted field where he told her to kneel, and then smashed in the side of her head with a shovel.

He left her half-buried; a dog walker interrupted him and he fled. His intention was to leave the area, but he didn't want to go without his daughter. That afternoon, he tried to pick her up from school. Unfortunately for Douglas, a neighbor had seen his car a few times on the Seldons' street while he was planning the crime, and had reported his license plate to the Bloomfield Hills police. The dog walker found Claire's body and called it in, so when Douglas made a commotion at Jessie's school when they wouldn't let him take her (he wasn't on the approved list) and the principal called the police, there was already a bulletin out on him in connection with the murder. When he was captured, he confessed at once, but then retracted when his trial started.

Despite what were clearly complicating mental issues, he was, as Jessie had said, declared competent to stand trial. He was given life in prison.

Preuss interrupted his reading to meet with his two o'clock appointment, then afterward spent an hour on the phone. He finally got through to Detective Michael Luedke from the Bloomfield Hills Police Department, whom Preuss had met after 9/11 during a local terrorism training session. From Luedke, Preuss learned two facts: Both detectives who had led the original Claire Seldon investigation for the Bloomfield Hills Police two decades before were dead, and the Seldons' business was still active in Ferndale.

That was the place to start.

A two-story brick building on the east side of Ferndale was headquarters for the Johnson Manufacturing Corp. The rear of the site was taken up by imposing metal storage silos and semi trailers. He parked in a guest parking spot and made his way through a gate in the chain link fence that surrounded the grounds.

The receptionist buzzed him inside and asked him which Mr. Seldon he wanted to see. "How many are there?" he asked.

"Well," she said, "there's Lawrence Seldon, CEO of the corporation. But he's out of town at the moment. Then there's Malcolm

Seldon. He's chief financial officer. There's also William Seldon. He's the former CEO."

"He's actually the one I wanted to speak with. He's not in?"

"He doesn't keep an office on-site any more. He's retired."

"Living the good life?"

She shrugged, unwilling to comment.

"Is he still in Bloomfield Hills?"

"Sorry, I can't release that information."

"Fair enough. If he's not in, I'll speak with Malcolm Seldon."

"Do you have an appointment?"

"No," he said. Once he could have flashed a shield and gotten instant access, but now he had to go through more pedestrian channels. He gave her a business card, and said, "I'm a private investigator."

"May I tell him what this is regarding?"

"I'd rather speak about it directly with Mr. Seldon."

She gave him a twitch of annoyance and opened a line on the desk telephone and murmured into her headset, casting him a glance to let him know she was talking about him, and not in the most complimentary terms.

She disconnected and said, "If you'll have a seat, someone will be with you shortly."

He thanked her and sat in a chrome and leather chair beside a massive ficus plant in the waiting area. It looked real, but when he felt the slippery leaves he saw it was a clever imitation.

On the table beside him was a copy of a glossy four-page brochure about the company. He read through the short—and, he was certain, sanitized and romanticized—history of the organization.

Johnson Manufacturing Corp., he read, was begun by Curtis Johnson, a chemical engineer. Johnson developed a process for manufacturing nerve gas during the Second World War to compete with the Germans' program. Though the process was never used, Johnson adapted it after the war to manufacture and distill industrial solvents; this appeared to be the source of the company's (and family's) wealth. Johnson Manufacturing was based in Ferndale but had locations in Brazil, Mexico, and across Europe.

The company was a third-generation family-owned business; William Seldon, Johnson's son-in-law, a chemical engineer, retired early, the history claimed, in order to turn the company over to the next generation of Seldons "to ensure a continuing stable and prosperous future for the organization."

Preuss read about their vision (to grow in the marketplace), their mission (to be the world's preferred provider of chemical products), their quality policy (a constant commitment to excellence), and their environmental policy (to meet or exceed applicable laws, regulations, and requirements). There were thumbnail photos of Johnson and the Seldon men.

In the photos, Curtis Johnson was a round-headed, unsmiling, stiff-necked old bird. Seldon looked like a smooth-talker, oozing charm with dark wavy hair and matinee idol good looks. The two Seldon brothers, Lawrence and Malcolm, had their father's features except for the small, predatory eyes on both young men. Born to privilege, those eyes saw the world as prey.

After he had been waiting forty-five minutes, Preuss strolled over to the receptionist. She was busy answering the phones and ignored him.

When she hung up from her call, he said, "Still waiting."

She looked up and did an exaggerated double take, as if surprised he were still there even though he had been sitting six feet from her the entire time.

Without a word to him, she connected a call on her desk set and murmured into her headset again.

She disconnected. "If you could hang on a few more minutes?"

Instead of sitting back down, he walked around the waiting area, where photos of the international facilities were displayed on the walls, prominently featuring tanker trucks and palm trees.

After another ten minutes, a squat, husky man strode through a set of glass double doors and approached Preuss with his hand outstretched. He had a round bald head and dark fringe of hair above prominent ears. Preuss recognized Malcolm Seldon. He was a few inches shorter than Preuss and had added pounds and lost hair since his photo had been taken for the promotional brochure. He was looking more like his grandfather than his father. In person, and with the extra weight, he didn't look as carnivorous as he did in his earlier photographs.

"Sorry to keep you waiting," he said. "Mal Seldon."

Preuss returned his handshake. "Thanks for seeing me." He handed Seldon a business card.

"Come this way."

Seldon led the way back through the double doors, which he opened with a fob on his keyring. Preuss followed him through a narrow corridor with office cubicles on either side. The smell of acetone was harsh. It stung Preuss's eyes and made his nose run.

Seldon spoke over his shoulder as he walked. "Crazy day today. My brother's in Mexico City. We're bringing a new process online down there. Still working the bugs out."

A sign on the wall read, "Executive Suite," with an arrow pointing up a set of stairs. An elevator stood open beside the stairs. "Stairs okay?" Seldon asked.

"Fine."

The chemical odor diminished on the second floor, which was carpeted with a plush beige pile. Historical photos of the company's development lined the walls. Early black and white blow-ups showed founder Curtis Johnson in an old-fashioned leather apron at work at a chemical lab bench. He was small and sour-looking, and gazed out at the cameras with ill-disguised annoyance.

Must have been a delight to work for, Preuss thought.

Other photos showed William Seldon, by himself and with Curtis and Lawrence and Malcolm. There was a family portrait of the Seldon men and their spouses and children, all sitting outside in a park, clean-cut and well-dressed, the perfect All-American extended family. In the photo, a glossy brunette sat beside a greying William Seldon. Evidently his second wife, since the photo seemed relatively recent.

Now Malcolm Seldon led him into a large office with a chocolate leather sofa and chairs at one end and a massive wooden desk at the other. Seldon held out a hand toward the sofa. Preuss sat and Seldon took one of the chairs.

"Can I get you something?" Seldon asked. "Coffee, a soft drink?" He spoke slowly, with an elaborately calm manner.

"No thanks," Preuss said, "I'm good."

"Okay. So, Mr.—?"

"Preuss," he prompted.

"What can we do for you? Sheila said you wanted to talk to my father?"

"I do."

"He's been retired for some time."

"So she said. I'm looking into the death of your father's first wife, Claire. She was your mother?"

"Yes," Seldon said. He sat back and his demeanor abruptly changed. A squirrelly agitation replaced the businessman's even temper. He opened his suit coat and began smoothing his tie over the bulge of his belly.

"Well," Seldon said, "excuse me for saying this, but what's to look into? The guy who did it was found a long time ago."

"There are a few loose ends," Preuss said.

"At this late date?"

"Yes."

"Like what?"

"To start with, did you know the man who was convicted? Raymond Douglas."

Seldon shook his head. "Never met him."

"But you saw him at the trial?"

"Of course. But not to speak to. It was a terrible time. Just terrible. It wasn't bad enough we all had to be in court every day for the trial, but everything was reported in the papers and on TV in excruciating detail. Look," Seldon said, "can I ask what this is about? What are you trying to find out?"

"It's come to light the man who killed your mother may have had help."

Seldon frowned. "But he was found guilty on his own."

"Have you ever heard of anyone else being in the picture?"

"Absolutely not."

"How old were you at the time?"

"Twenty-three. My brother was twenty-five. Our sister was . . . let's see, she's the baby . . . she was twenty."

"Your sister?"

"Yes. Mary."

A young woman had not appeared in any of the family portraits, nor was she mentioned in any descriptions of the company. "Is she in the family business, too?"

"No. Mary and our mother were very close," he said, as if that explained the sister's exclusion. "Mary took Mom's death pretty hard."

Preuss waited for Seldon to say more, but the other man was silent.

Finally Seldon shook his head. "You know, I think you better talk to my brother when he comes back."

"Why is that?"

"He's always been the spokesman for the family when it comes to our mother's . . . situation. I'm a bit uncomfortable talking about it. Especially where our sister's concerned."

"Why?"

More smoothing of the necktie.

"During the trial, we decided it would be best if we presented a single face to the world. As the oldest, my brother took on that role. And he's been doing it ever since."

Preuss considered that. "When's he due back?"

"He just left this morning. He said he might be home as early as tonight or tomorrow morning."

"Would you give him my card and ask him to call me when he gets in?"

"Absolutely," Seldon said. He was visibly relieved to be close to the end of this conversation.

"Nothing else you can tell me?" Preuss asked.

"No. But," Seldon said, holding up Preuss's card, "I'll make sure my brother gets in touch as soon as he's back."

5

"Rhonda tells me we might have a new client," Manny Greene said.

"After a fashion," Preuss said. "One hitch. She's dead."

Sitting at the table in his conference room in the firm's offices, Manny took a thoughtful sip of the coffee he had just brewed from the beans he roasted himself. He bought the beans online from a company that imported organic beans from Ethiopia that were reputed to be the best coffee beans in the world. Manny was serious about his coffee.

He smacked his lips and savored the taste. He sat in the jacket of his suit, dove grey with a muted plaid and a lilac and blue striped silk tie. A paisley handkerchief peeked demurely out of his breast pocket. Manny never removed his jacket in the office during business hours, though he did concede to unbuttoning it before he sat down.

"I'd call that a hitch," he agreed.

Manny was an 84-year-old private detective who had primarily worked on accident investigations for one of the local attorneys who specialized in accidents and social security rejections. He had been after Preuss to join him in a partnership, but Preuss at first said no; when he retired from the Detective Bureau, Preuss wanted to leave this kind of work behind. But after admitting to himself it was what he most loved to do and was best at, he finally agreed to Manny's offer. So far, the arrangement was working well.

Sitting in his shirtsleeves with his tie undone, Preuss explained the circumstances of Jessie Douglas's project, including what amounted to her bequest of the retainer.

Sitting to his right, Rhonda Citron said, "The credit card number belongs to a Renee Cacavelli. Still trying to track her down.

There seem to be a lot of charges on this card. But they've all been paid off promptly."

"So here's where we are," Preuss said. "Assuming the charge will be honored and paid, I thought I'd essentially work off the retainer, and start to do what she asked me to."

Knowing in his heart he was going to do this anyway. But the retainer fee gave him cover.

Manny, who rarely missed anything, watched Preuss with his unblinking stare. "Think there's anything here?"

Preuss shrugged. "We'll find out."

"Even if it turns out the charges won't be approved," Manny said, "which we won't know till we talk to whoever's name is on the card, maybe you should keep working this a little more."

"Sounds good," Preuss said, giving Manny a knowing nod. "Rhonda, can you do some background checks on the Seldon family? Father, first wife, second wife, three kids?"

"Will do."

Based on their hourly rate of $100 and the retainer of $1,500 that Jessie Douglas paid, the three decided the dead woman had bought approximately fifteen hours of Preuss's time.

After their meeting, Preuss returned to his office and reviewed the Douglas court documents for several more hours, then left for the day. He stopped for Chinese takeout at Hong Kong 1 on Nine Mile and kept reading the transcripts at home for another hour.

When his headache returned, he stowed what was left of his General Tso's chicken in the refrigerator and set out for Toby's.

Toby lay back in the reclining chair in his room at the group home. When he heard his father's voice, he perked up and turned a round chubby face in Preuss's direction. He gave Preuss a crooked smile with a sweet, slightly goofy gap between his two front teeth.

Toby had been putting on weight lately and was getting pudgier. He didn't have the chance to do any exercise, since he couldn't walk with his cerebral palsy. And he couldn't care for his daily needs, including feeding himself, so his nurses gave him a fill-up every four hours with a can of his formula pumped directly into his g-tube. There really wasn't any way for him to lose weight; Preuss would talk to the nutrition specialist the next time Toby had an appointment and ask if his calorie intake might be reduced.

Preuss put his arms around his son and held the boy close. Toby at first squirmed but then relaxed with the deep pressure of his father's arms. Preuss inhaled the boy's scent, a mixture of sweat, urine, and what was left of the deodorant his morning aide had jammed under his tight arms.

"Need a change?" Preuss asked. He lifted the waistband of Toby's shorts and saw the blue stripes that indicated his diaper was full of pee.

Preuss negotiated the overhead sling on its curved track so it was directly above Toby's chair, then pressed the button that lowered the crosspiece. Preuss fastened four S-hooks dangling on chains at the end of the crosspiece to Toby's sling, and when he made sure the boy was secure Preuss pressed the button to lift Toby up, smiling and humming with pleasure at his ascension.

Preuss lowered his son in bed and shifted and tugged and rolled the boy until he got the soggy diaper off, wiped him clean, and wrestled the new diaper on. He pulled Toby's shorts back up over the hump of diaper and then sat his son up on the side of his bed.

Preuss sat next to him with an arm around the boy's narrow back. Now that he was putting on some weight, the bones of Toby's shoulders were not as prominent as they used to be. He still had stick-thin legs, since he never bore any weight on them.

In the beginning of September, Toby would be twenty-one. So hard to believe his sweet, vulnerable boy was growing so fast . . . When Toby was an infant, the doctors told Preuss and Jeanette that Toby probably wouldn't live past his twenties. Preuss hoped they were as wrong about that as they seemed to be about most things having to do with his son.

Toby leaned into his father and nuzzled against Preuss's chest. Toby snuffled and rubbed, leaving a little wet spot of spit and snot on his father's shirt. Preuss whispered, "I love you very much," into his son's hair, and rocked him gently from side to side. Toby hummed his own reply, which Preuss chose to interpret as, "I love you, too, Dad."

Preuss got Toby settled into his wheelchair, and they walked up to a diner in the Berkley shopping area on Twelve Mile Road to get out of the heat. Preuss went through the usual "He doesn't eat" routine with the server, ordered coffee, and chatted quietly with his son about their days. As always, Toby added vocalizations that Preuss took as actual speech acts and incorporated into his monologue.

Then they walked toward the two music stores in Berkley. Preuss wheeled Toby into one of the stores and the boy immediately brightened at the sounds of electric guitars wailing in the practice room and, playing separate rhythms, a drum kit in the display area. The instruments were competing rather than combining into a single tune, but Toby didn't care. He added his voice to the mix, screeching in a high falsetto as though trying to sing to both instruments at the same time.

The store manager, a big guy with a full scruffy beard and pony tail who knew Preuss and Toby from their previous trips, came over, knelt down to say hi to Toby, and went to get the guitar strings Preuss asked for.

When they finished that errand, Preuss pushed Toby further up Twelve Mile, and then turned around and walked back down to Toby's street. They returned to the group home, where Preuss gave his son a bath, got him ready for bed, and put on the Judy Collins albums that Toby used to relax at night. Toby hummed along with the songs for a while, until the lids over his almond-shaped brown eyes first flickered and then closed as he sank into sleep.

Preuss stayed for a while longer, watching Toby sleep with his heart filled with love for his son. When the last Judy Collins song ended, Preuss roused himself, leaned over to give the boy a gentle kiss goodbye on Toby's temple, and slipped out of the quiet group home.

Back at his house in Ferndale, he made a cup of decaf and took it out to the deck off his dining room to sit in one of the aluminum chairs. It was 9:30, with a glow of light still in the sky, though a layer of puffy violet clouds hid any stars.

He drank his coffee and tried to empty his mind of the commotion of the day. He didn't succeed. He heard the echoes of all the voices—Malcom Seldon's, Shelley Larkin's, Reg Trombley's—clashing like the guitars and drums at the music store, each voice singing a different tune.

He closed his eyes, inhaled the sweet smell of a July evening, listened to the crickets chirruping in the bushes. A summer night in friendly Ferndale.

His thoughts went back to other nights, other years, when his house was fuller and on nights like this the backyard was rocking with activity, even at this hour . . . Jason shooting hoops with his friends long after the sun went down, his wife Jeanette sitting next to him chatting on the phone, and a younger and smaller Toby in his large umbrella stroller parked on the deck between his father and mother, shaking the red rings he loved to hold.

Well . . . Even as he thought about this scene, Preuss knew he was fabricating it out of a sense of false nostalgia. This hour would have been too late for Toby to stay up, so he would already have been asleep; Jason more often than not would have been at someone else's home; and Jeanette would not have been sitting next to him but would have been down at the fence, chatting with the neighbors, or more likely inside the house, watching television or reading upstairs.

Preuss himself would have been outside, by himself, drinking something considerably stronger than decaf coffee.

Wondering, as now, what had happened to his life.

Now things were even worse than they had been back then. His wife was dead, his older son was gone, and all he had left was his beloved Toby, who lived somewhere else.

A line from a poem he had read in college popped into his head: *Where is the life we have lost in living?* He couldn't remember where it came from—one of the English classes he had taken when he briefly thought of becoming an English major (an intention he abandoned in about a second when he realized he would have to take courses with his mother, who was an English professor at Eastern Michigan University, where he had started college).

His random thoughts drifted to Shelley Larkin and their troubled past, then to Jessie Douglas, abandoned in a dumpster. With no present or future, troubled or otherwise.

Where is the life she lost in dying? he wondered. And who stole that life? How close was Reg Trombley to finding out?

More voices . . .

He opened his eyes, finished his coffee, drank in the fragrance of the summer night one last time, and went back inside the house.

Tuesday, July 17, 2012

6

Mid-morning, Rhonda appeared in his doorway.

"There's a Lawrence Seldon on the phone. Are you in?"

"I am."

"Transferring."

In a few moments, Preuss's office phone rang. "Martin Preuss."

"Mr. Preuss," said the man's voice. Deep, mellifluous, breezy, practiced at being in charge. "Larry Seldon here. You spoke with my brother yesterday."

"I did."

"You have questions about the man who killed our mother?"

"I do. Can we meet? I'd like to go over some things with you."

"My schedule's pretty tight," Seldon said. "I'm afraid I wouldn't have the time. Besides, as far as I'm concerned, this was settled a long time ago. I wouldn't have anything else to add."

On a hunch, Preuss said, "I'm especially anxious to talk about your sister," to see what would happen.

He waited.

"My sister?"

"Yes."

The magic words. After another pause, Seldon said, "I might be able to fit you in. It'd have to be soon. When can you get here?"

"Half an hour."

"I'll move a meeting. See you in a half hour. Please don't be late."

Lawrence Seldon matched his voice. He was a trim, strapping man—Preuss guessed him to be a few inches over six feet—with his father's glossy good looks and long dark hair swept back from a handsome face tanned to the reddish-copper color of a new penny. His handshake was crushing. He ushered Preuss into a vast conference room lined with plaques and awards the company had won. On shelves Preuss could also see trophies in the shape of footballs on stands.

"I won those," Seldon said.

Preuss made a noncommittal sound.

"I was a wide receiver at U of M. All-American my senior year. Got a tryout with the Jets, but I decided on the family business instead."

Preuss thought of all the people he knew who had gone to the University of Michigan in Ann Arbor, and how most of them made sure you knew that fact within five minutes of meeting them. Add Lawrence Seldon to that list.

Seldon sat at the head of the conference table. Preuss took the chair next to him. On the wall opposite was a blown-up grainy black and white photo of Seldon on a tennis court, crouching intently as though in the second before a serve came his way, with headband, wristbands, and short shorts.

"I asked my brother to sit in with us," Seldon said. "He'll be here in a minute."

"Fine."

Seldon examined the business card Preuss had given him. "Private investigations," he read.

"Yes."

Seldon tapped the card on the table. "What's your business with my sister?"

Before Preuss could answer, Malcolm Seldon entered the conference room. He shook hands with Preuss and took a chair next to his brother on the other side of the table from where Preuss sat. Seeing them side-by-side, Preuss was struck by how much Malcolm looked like a shorter, overweight, blowzy, balder version of his brother, even though he was younger than Lawrence.

"I was just asking Mr. Preuss here what his business is with Mary," Seldon explained.

Malcolm nodded and smoothed his tie over his belly.

"My agency has been hired to look into the circumstances of your mother's death," Preuss said.

"By whom?"

"That's confidential."

"For what reason?"

"I'm filling in some background."

"And you thought that gave you permission to pry into my family?"

"I'm trying to get a sense of who's who in the Raymond Douglas case."

"That still doesn't explain what you want from my sister," Lawrence said. Malcolm kept silent.

"I'm speaking with all the principals," Preuss said. "Your brother told me your sister took your mother's death particularly hard."

"We all did," Seldon said. "It was a terrible tragedy. I'll ask you again, sir, what's your interest in my sister?"

Without letting Preuss respond, Seldon said, "Look—the man who killed my mother was arrested and given a life sentence. What do you hope to gain from this"—he held up Preuss's business card and flicked it as though it was on fire and he was trying to put out the flame—"all these years later?"

"I have reason to believe he may have had an accomplice who was never found."

"Ridiculous," Lawrence Seldon said. "And you can't possibly think Mary had anything to do with our mother's death?"

"This is a routine part of the investigation. I'd like to hear what she has to say."

"I'm not sure I see the need for that. In fact, I won't allow it."

Won't allow it. Sounds like he's more than just a spokesman for the family, Preuss thought.

"Is there something you don't want me to find, Mr. Seldon?"

"I'm just afraid you're going to go barging around and reopen wounds that haven't healed. Especially for my sister, even after all these years."

Preuss said nothing.

Seldon regarded him. He held Preuss's business card between thumb and forefinger and flexed the cardboard. He seemed to be reconsidering his approach.

"Listen," he said, more conversationally now, just two guys talking, "after my mother's death—our mother's death," he said, including Malcolm for the first time, "Mary . . . Well, she went off the deep end, if I can put it that way."

"I'm not sure what that means."

"It means she fell into a deep, deep depression after our mother was killed. She got involved with drugs, she got mixed up with some awful people who took advantage of her . . . Things went very badly for her for a long time. Frankly, I'm not sure she ever recovered. And that's why I'd prefer you leave her out of whatever it is you're doing. She's had a hard time, and it's left her very fragile. She's just not strong enough to stand up to your questions about all this. Even after all these years."

"I appreciate that. But she should be the one to tell me that."

Seldon shook his head. "*I'm* telling you. I'm trying to protect my family, sir. Please understand that. And leave her out of this. Any questions you have, you can ask me."

"Okay," Preuss said. "Did you know Raymond Douglas?"

"No."

"How about Jessie Douglas?"

"I have no idea who that is."

"Raymond's daughter."

"How would I possibly know her?"

"She's been around lately asking about her father."

"Never heard of her."

"And she was just killed two nights ago."

Seldon leaned forward with his elbows on the table. He steepled his fingertips. "I'm sorry to hear that, of course," he said. "But I don't know her. And it's nothing to do with me. Or any of my family. Let me remind you, we're the victims here. It was our family that suffered from that psychopathic murderer. As I told you over the phone, there's nothing more to add to the facts of the case. Now if there's nothing else, please excuse me. I have a multimillion dollar international business to run."

Preuss said, "If there is anything to the allegation someone else is involved in the killing of your mother, I should think your family would want to know the truth."

Seldon sat back in his chair and swallowed an angry outburst. He exchanged a look with Malcolm. He ran a hand over his perfect hair and fixed Preuss with a distasteful scowl.

"Mr. Preuss," Lawrence Seldon said finally, "we already know the truth. The best thing you can do for my family is this: Go away. And leave us in peace."

7

In the end, Seldon refused to tell Preuss where his sister Mary lived, or give him any further information about his mother's case. It would take Rhonda Citron five seconds to find the address for Mary Seldon, but Preuss left Seldon's office wondering what the source of Seldon's animosity was. Was he really trying to protect his sister's privacy, or did he have something to hide? Or was he just annoyed at the case being opened again, even informally?

Or he could have been put off because Preuss didn't seem cowed by his bluster?

Preuss was about to pull out of the guest parking lot when he spotted Malcolm Seldon exiting the rear door of the building. Suit jacket billowing behind him, Seldon hurried over to a black Lexus in the employee parking lot. He jumped in and the car roared out of the lot and went south on Wanda toward Eight Mile.

Preuss decided to follow.

At the corner of Eight Mile, Seldon turned right and headed toward Woodward. Preuss waited till he could shoot out through a break in traffic and wound up several cars behind Seldon.

Seldon turned right onto Woodward and took it all the way up to veer right on Adams, in Birmingham. He turned right on Maple and made a left onto Eton on the other side of the railroad viaduct. About a mile up the road, he made a u-turn and pulled over in front of a two-story brick building with two tall white colonnades on either side of the front entrance.

Seldon trotted up to the front door of the building and went inside.

Preuss continued up Eton and turned around where the street dead-ended. He drove back and parked down the block behind Seldon's car.

Then he waited.

A half hour later, Seldon rushed out of the building and sped off in the Lexus. He looked as agitated coming out as he had going in.

Preuss waited a few minutes to make sure Seldon wasn't coming back, then moved the Explorer up to where Seldon had parked. He walked to the front of the building. The exterior door was unlocked, and a plate on the right wall of the inside foyer held names typed in tiny squares beside buttons.

He pressed the buzzer for Seldon, #103.

In a few seconds, the interior door buzzed. He pushed it open and went up two steps. Down the hall, a door opened. "What did you forget?" a woman's voice said.

When Preuss came into view, she stiffened. "Who are you?"

She was a tall woman, as tall as Preuss, with a careworn elegance and black hair worn short, almost shaven, except for a fashionable lock that swept down across one side of her face. Her eyes were deep set, and she had parentheses of worry on each side of her mouth. Her face was puffy, as though she had been crying. Her brother Malcolm said she was twenty when her mother died; that would make her forty. She looked ten years older.

"Mary Seldon?"

"Who's asking?"

"Martin Preuss." He handed her a business card.

"Ah," she said, "it's you."

"Your brother told you about me?"

"Both of them."

"Can we speak for a few minutes?"

"About what?"

"Your mother."

She held his gaze without answering.

"Did your brother tell you not to speak with me?" Preuss asked, ready to explain why she should talk with him.

"Of course," she said. "They both did. But when has listening to my brothers ever been a good idea?"

8

She poured him a cup of coffee. "I hope you don't take sugar," she said. "I'm diabetic and don't keep any in the house. Can't stand those sugar substitutes, either."

"Black is fine," Preuss said.

"And I rarely have any visitors, so . . ."

She sat across from him at her dining room table.

"Why did your brothers tell you not to talk to me, Mary?"

"It was Lolly more than Mal. He said don't talk to you under any circumstances."

"Lolly?"

"Sorry, that's the family nickname for Larry. When he was little, he couldn't pronounce his name. It always came out as Lolly."

Preuss said nothing.

"He said you met with him this morning," Mary said.

"I did. Not long ago."

"He called me right after you left, then. He *ordered* me not to talk to you. He must have sent Mal to make sure I didn't. His usual errand boy."

She knocked a Newport out of a pack she drew from her pocket. "You mind?"

"Your house, your rules," Preuss said.

"Yeah, I know. But still." She lit up, took a deep draw, blew it out in a blue cloud of smoke that curled over the table. Her hand shook as she flicked the lighter. She caught Preuss noticing it, but didn't comment.

In the living room, a tiny shaggy Shih Tzu raised its head from where it lay on a doggy bed on the carpet, all bristly beige facial fur and squashed black snout and snaggletoothed underbite. "That's But-ton," Mary said. "He won't bother you. Not unless you trip over him."

Satisfied nothing out of the ordinary was happening, Button let his head fall back between his front paws and heaved a grunt of satisfaction.

"Good boy," Mary told the animal.

Preuss watched the look of affection Mary gave the dog. Maybe I should get a dog, he thought. Toby hated to have his face touched, and particularly hated to have it licked by a dog. But Preuss could train the dog not to lick, and a dog might be a good companion for them both . . .

"My brother's been trying to tell me what to do my whole life," Mary said.

"He told you I'm looking into your mother's death?"

"Yes. But I'm not sure how I can help."

"I'm asking whether someone else was involved besides the man who was convicted. Raymond Douglas."

She chewed that over. "Everybody said he did it on his own."

"I have information that says otherwise."

"Wait—are you saying he didn't kill my mother?"

"No, he's guilty, that's certain. But there may have been an-other person connected with the crime. I know the outlines of what happened, through the trial transcripts, but I'm hoping you can fill in some of the details for me."

She thought about that for several seconds. Then she said, "I know Lolly told me not to talk to you about this. But I really would rather not discuss it. It was all very hard on me. It's still hard to talk about."

"Fair enough."

"Sorry."

"Your brother told me your mother's death hit you very hard."

"*Very* hard? Does that mean it hit either one of them hard at all? Did they even notice she was gone?"

She tapped her cigarette on the edge of an ashtray. "Okay, that's not fair," she said. "I can't say it didn't affect them. But they seemed to get over it right away. Not me." She looked at him. "I was devastated when she died. I had to drop out of college. I went sort of crazy for a while. I was a mess. At some point along the way, I even had a baby."

She took a deep draw on the cigarette.

"When I found out I was pregnant, I was at my lowest. I considered killing myself, that's how down I was. I couldn't take care of myself, how could I possibly take care of a baby? But Lolly saved me, I have to give him that. If he hadn't been there, if I hadn't had him to be concerned about me and take charge of things, I'd be dead by now. I have no doubt whatsoever. And who knows how my son would have turned out."

"Where is he now?"

"My son? In New York. Matt, his name is. Goes to NYU. Wants to be an actor, so he's putting in his dues as a waiter during the summer."

Expensive school, Preuss thought. He looked around at the simple furnishings, the baskets and ceramic vases on end tables and shelves, cluttered but none of it shouting ostentatious wealth.

As though reading his mind, she said, "It costs a fortune to send him there, but Lolly's taking care of it."

As if remembering her brother's generosity, she softened toward him. "I suppose Lolly thinks keeping you away from me is in my best interest," she said. "Thinks he's protecting me, as usual."

"It must have worked," Preuss said. "You seem to be doing well. Your son is doing well."

"Wasn't easy, believe me. I think my son raised me as much as I raised him. It's not pretty when a child has to parent his mother."

"No," Preuss agreed. Not pretty at all, as he well knew. His father had been an alcoholic, and he would never allow his children to parent him, neither Preuss nor his older brother. Preuss's father barely allowed Preuss's mother to care for him, or for the children either, for that matter; between a disinterested and addicted father, a distracted mother, and an older brother with his own monster drug problem, Preuss basically raised himself. For better or worse.

"Matt found me passed out in my own puke more times than I care to remember," Mary Seldon continued. "But he stood by me. He picked me up, cleaned me off. And he always knew I loved him, no matter how low I sank. Matt never knew his father. I barely remember him, he passed in and out of my life so fast. I barely remember that time at all, tell you the truth. For about ten years after my mother died, I was a lost soul."

"And now?"

"I stopped drinking. And doing drugs. Stopped all my bad habits. I still have some aftereffects, though."

She held up her hand so he could notice the tremor.

"Neurological damage. I was in a fire once, too stoned to get out. I may have even started it, can't remember. Smoke inhalation damaged my brain, left me with the shakes. I never did go back to school, but once I got my feet under me, I started working for the company. Lolly gave me the job. Public relations."

She gave Preuss a tight, bitter smile. "That's where they put you in a family business when you don't have any other skills, right? Lolly kept me on way longer than he should have. I finally left on my own . . . I was terrible at it. Didn't feel like faking it any more."

She took another long pull on her cigarette and blew it out over her shoulder, away from Preuss.

"Lolly makes sure I get what he calls a consultant's retainer from the business, but really it's an allowance to help me make ends meet. Pretty sure it also helps assuage his guilt."

"What's he feel guilty for?"

She shook her head. "No, that's wrong. It doesn't *assuage* his guilt, it's *in lieu of* his guilt."

"Over what?"

"Over why he bounced back so fast after our mother's death. Lolly and Mal both. They just went right on like it was a bump in the road. I don't know if it's because they didn't have any feelings about her because my father turned them against her, or because he taught them not to show their feelings so well they may as well not have had any. He raised them like little Marines in boot camp and he was their DI—complete with verbal abuse and beatings. They quaked in his presence. I don't mean to sound ungrateful, because Lolly's done so much for me. But my father?"

She shook her head. "Not a nice man."

"How'd he take your mother's death?"

She scoffed. "He was remarried before my mother'd been dead a year. What does that tell you about how he took it?"

"Have you talked to him lately?"

"Not in years. And I don't intend to talk to him again anytime soon, either."

9

On the way back to Southfield, he wondered how reliable Mary Seldon was. Though she claimed to be sober, she was still under the influence of abiding anger at her father and conflicted feelings about her brothers. Preuss didn't know how much that would skew her perspective.

And despite what her older brother had said, she seemed anything but fragile. On the contrary, her anger gave her a kind of steel. So why was Lawrence—Lolly—trying to keep him away?

Rhonda Citron was seated at her desk when he entered the offices of Greene and Preuss, Investigations. She gave him a handful of phone message slips. "These came in while you were out, you popular guy."

He thanked her and helped himself to a cup of Manny's special coffee and settled himself in his office with the door closed. He sorted through the message slips. One was from Brendan Flynn, his bandmate in the Flynns, the group Preuss sat in with on rhythm guitar from time to time, letting him know there was a new gig scheduled for Labor Day. The other messages were for cases he had in progress: The pre-employment background check, a case of embezzlement from a local restaurant, and a skip trace.

Previously, Manny turned down those kinds of jobs because he ran a one-man agency and didn't have time to pursue opportunities. Now that Preuss was with him, he had the ability to expand the agency caseload. Though he and Preuss had agreed they would still turn down the skeevy investigative work, like following cheating spouses.

Preuss called Brendan Flynn back first and said to plan on him for the gig. Brendan told him they were starting to schedule rehearsals, and Preuss said to let him know when they were and he'd arrange to be there. He also marked the gig on his calendar and made a note to tell Toby's house about it; whenever he could, he took Toby with him when he played, which meant the group home would have to arrange for an aide to accompany Toby.

He worked through the other calls, then took a sip of coffee and thought about his meetings with the Seldon sibs. What he really needed to do now was speak with the paterfamilias—the family drill instructor, as Mary had called him.

He went online and found the phone number and address for William Seldon in Bloomfield Hills. He googled the address and saw it was on a cul-de-sac on Orange Lake, one of the cluster of small lakes up near Pontiac.

"My husband's around somewhere," the woman said. "I think he's out walking the dog."

Preuss and Christine Seldon sat in facing chairs in the den of the Seldons' sprawling one-story home in the deep woods of the wealthy northern suburb. She looked at him and smiled; she had a unique smile, her mouth wide open as if she were having the best time ever and were just about to give out with a raucous laugh that would shake the walls. She was tanned and robust, with lustrous auburn hair and lively eyes, the kind that could with a straight face be called "sparkling."

A picture window on the rear wall looked out on a wooded backyard; beside it a door led outside. The other walls were lined with bookshelves filled with hardbacks and oversized art tomes. The room was so large it made the gleaming ebony grand piano in the corner look tiny.

Christine Seldon noticed Preuss looking at it and said, "Do you play?"

"No. Just admiring it. Beautiful instrument."

"Indeed it is. Bill gave that to me for our fifth wedding anniversary."

She stood in one graceful move and swept across the room to sit at the piano bench. She opened the keyboard cover and fired off a showy classical run. She segued into the opening bars of "Rhapsody in Blue." She was a strong and confident player, proud of her ability.

She stopped abruptly and closed the keyboard cover and turned to face him with her full-wattage smile. Take that, mister, her manner said.

"Very impressive," he said, playing his role.

"Thanks." She returned to her chair. "I come from a generation when every young lady was expected to play the piano."

"I'd say that's more than just playing piano. You got some serious chops. Ever played professionally?"

She smoothed her hair in acknowledgment. "I played a little when I was younger." She gave him a flirtatious wink, as though they were both in on the joke of her immodest humility.

From somewhere in the house a door slammed, and he heard a dog barking and the tapping of claws on wooden floors.

"There's Bill now," she said. "With Bandit."

In another few moments, a man appeared in the doorway from the dining room with a rambunctious German Shepherd. The man was tall and thin and stooped, with wispy white hair windswept over his balding head. Preuss found it hard to find a trace of the smiling, confident man he had once been in the photos from Johnson Manufacturing; the craggy figure of William Seldon who stood in the doorway looked more befuddled than commanding.

The German Shepherd tore its leash from Seldon's hand and gamboled around the room, coming to rest with his nose in Preuss's crotch. Bandit looked up at him with merry brown eyes.

Preuss thought again about getting a dog. As though picking up his thoughts, Bandit wagged his tail happily. See how much fun we are? he seemed to say.

"Bandit!" Christine Seldon said. Her husband stood where he was.

"Bandit, no!" the woman shouted. "Sorry," she told Preuss.

The dog withdrew his snout and made another lap around the room, this time flopping to rest at William Seldon's feet.

"No!" Seldon cried. "Bad dog!"

Bandit looked up at him with a vulpine smile.

Christine said, "Bill, pick up his leash and come around here. Sit next to me." She patted the cushion of the love seat beside her chair.

Seldon did as he was told, reining in the high-spirited animal as he moved over.

"Bill," Christine said, "this gentleman is Martin Preuss."

Seldon ignored Preuss and, scowling, focused on getting Bandit down at his feet. "Lie down! Lie down!" Bandit gave an unhappy groan, but followed the command.

Christine patted her husband's thigh. "Bill," she said, "this is Martin Preuss."

Seldon glanced at Preuss and gave him a distracted nod.

Christine turned to Preuss. "Now," she said, "on the phone you said you had some questions for us?"

"I'm looking into the death of Mr. Seldon's first wife. I hope you can help me."

She brought a hand full of rings to her neck. "Oh dear. Does this mean you're reopening the case?" For his part, William Seldon didn't seem to be paying attention. He was fussing with Bandit's leash, trying to unhook it from the dog's collar.

Preuss shook his head. "There are some questions about the man who was convicted."

Her eyes narrowed. "What kind of questions?"

"There's been an allegation he might not have been acting alone."

"There were *two* of them?"

"It's possible."

"But no one else was convicted, right?"

"Right."

"So what makes you think there was another person?"

Instead of answering, he said, "Had either of you heard anything about someone else being part of what happened?"

"Certainly not," Christine said.

Preuss turned to William Seldon. "How about you, Mr. Seldon?"

When Seldon didn't answer, or even acknowledge the question, Christine leaned forward and said, as though in confidence, "He's a bit hard of hearing."

Oh really, Preuss thought. Is that what you're calling it?

Preuss tapped Seldon on the knee to get his attention. The gesture did not go over well with Christine. She was about to reach out to deflect Preuss's hand, but caught herself. Another overprotective family member, he thought.

The older man looked up with his furry eyebrows drawn together.

"Mr. Seldon," Preuss said, more loudly, "did you ever hear about someone else being involved in the killing of your first wife, besides the man who was convicted?"

Seldon looked at Preuss with blank blue eyes, then turned to his wife as though for a hint.

"We haven't, have we, Bill?" Christine shook her head as she asked the question, cuing Seldon what answer she expected.

"No," he said. "No." He returned his attention to fiddling with Bandit's leash.

"There," Christine said. "You see? We're both convinced the right man was convicted of that awful crime."

"The issue isn't whether he's guilty or not, Mrs. Seldon. That's been established. The issue is whether he had help."

She clucked her tongue, as though in exasperation at Preuss's stupidity. "Wouldn't that have come out at the trial?"

"Not if Raymond Douglas kept it quiet. And the prosecutors and detectives didn't look any further."

"Did you ask them?"

"Unfortunately, they're no longer available. The detectives who worked the case are dead, so there's nobody to speak to about it. We just have the trial materials."

"And there's no mention of it there?"

"No."

"Well, there you have it," Christine said. She flashed her smile. "I wish we could help you."

He nodded and rose. "Thanks for your time. If you do think of something, please give me a call."

Bandit shot to his feet, ready to play.

"No!" Seldon cried. "Lie down! Lie down!"

The dog obeyed, and, chagrinned, rested his big head between his paws. He looked plaintively at Preuss.

Sorry, big guy, Preuss thought. Can't help you.

"I have your card," Christine said, patting the breast pocket of her blouse.

She led Preuss through the dining room, where a wall display of photographs and portraits showed the Seldons. In all of them, she was smiling her distinctive smile. In most, her husband was also smiling. In some, he had a kind of wry smirk as though amazed at his own good luck, while in others, a full-on joyful grin. Life was good.

There were also family photos and oil portraits of the Seldons and his two sons, grown up and looking grave. Mary Seldon didn't appear in any of them. One corner of the array held a few older black-and-white photos of a much younger William Seldon and a short, plain woman with clipped dark hair. Her mouth was a prim straight line, and her eyes were like two little black marbles.

"The first Mrs. Seldon?" Preuss asked.

"Yes. Claire." As she saw Preuss examining the photos, she said, "Bill loved her very much."

In all the photos of Bill and Claire, they were standing side-by-side without touching. In all the photos of Bill and Christine, they had their arms around each other, with their heads together, or with Christine's arm thrown around Bill's shoulder or across his knees. The easy intimacy of the gestures threw in sharp relief the stiff formality of the poses Bill and Claire struck.

"Her death was a great blow to him," Christine said.

Preuss made a noncommittal noise. "How did you two meet?"

"At a dinner party in New York City," she said. "We had mutual friends who introduced us. It was about a year after Claire passed. Bill was in town for business, and I lived on the upper east side. I'd lost my husband a few years before. We hit it off immediately, even though Bill was still grieving. And we've been together ever since."

She flashed him her open-mouthed smile, and with an arm on his shoulder guided him to a door off the room they were in. Not quite the bum's rush, but not an invitation to dawdle, either.

She opened the door for him, and before he stepped through she stopped him with a hand on his arm. "Mr. Preuss? Good luck with your investigation."

"Thanks."

"But unless you have something definite to tell us, I'll ask you not to mention any of this again. It upsets my husband. Okay?" She flashed him her glamorous smile before closing the door.

Interesting, he thought as he made his way down the long front walk to the driveway where he left the Explorer. That was essentially what Lawrence Seldon told him . . . Don't bother us. It's too upsetting.

Yet none of them looked upset—not the brothers, and not the elder Seldons. Only sister Mary seemed to bear the lingering scars of what had happened to their mother.

And Seldon himself seemed to be living on another planet entirely. Preuss wondered if he even remembered he was once married to a woman named Claire.

10

He spent an hour typing up notes from his interviews with all the Seldons. He had spoken with the whole family, except for the dead woman herself.

He caught himself. The first dead woman. There were now two dead women in the frame.

From his interviews with the Seldons, he had the sense of a group of people where each was trapped by his or her own needs: The father off pursuing his own pleasure with his happy and lively second wife, his two sons bogged down as the third generation trying to keep the family business afloat, and the daughter Mary lost in her grief.

And what of the mother? The victim of what had been judged a random crime—how did she fit into this family?

Preuss thought back to what he knew about Claire Seldon. He realized he didn't know much about her except in relation to the others . . . Daughter of the founder of the company, wife of the former CEO, mother of the current CEO and CFO, as well as the troubled Mary Seldon. But what of her personally?

Preuss remembered he had asked Rhonda to find some background information on Claire Seldon and her family.

He stuck his head out the door of his office. Rhonda was working away on her desktop computer.

"Rhonda," he said.

"What's up?"

"Remember I asked if you could put some information together about the Seldons?"

"Uh-huh?"

"Have you had a chance to do that? I'm especially interested in Claire Seldon."

"Not yet," she said. "Sorry. I started, but Manny had a couple of rush projects."

She reached across her desk and handed him a folder. "I got as far as finding out the name of Claire's best friend, but I haven't been able to make any more progress."

"You're the best. Thanks."

He took the folder into his office and closed the door. Claire's best friend was named Roxanne Stewart, with an address in Grosse Pointe Farms.

He called her number and got a standard impersonal answering service message. He left his name and phone number and told the woman he wanted to talk to her about Claire Seldon.

She called back immediately and apologized for not picking up because she didn't recognize his number. When he told her what he wanted, she said she wouldn't be able to meet with him until the next day, if that would be all right with him.

It would. She said she would be home all day till around five, so whenever he wanted to come would be fine.

So far, he had been focusing on Claire's family. But there was another side to this criminal equation. How much did he know about Raymond Douglas? If he did have an accomplice, it would have been someone he knew. What kind of connections did he have?

Preuss returned to the Douglas trial transcripts. He picked up where he had left off, but soon skipped around, scanning transcripts of the interviews with Raymond Douglas, as well as the detectives' notes on Douglas's background, in hopes of finding a useful direction.

He learned that Raymond Douglas had lived in Ferndale for most of his life. He went to Ferndale High School; a school psychologist there had even testified as a character witness for Douglas's doomed defense. A woman named Grace Portnoy, she had nothing but good things to say about Raymond when he was a youngster until his junior year in high school, when he started going off the rails. He skipped school, got in fights with other students, began accumulating a record of failed classes and petty crimes. He dropped out of school entirely after the eleventh grade. When he stole a car, the judge gave him a choice between joining the military or going to jail. Douglas chose the army.

So what was it that had turned the good kid into a bad seed? And from there to a psychotic killer? Did something happen in his junior year? Or was it his service in the military? Preuss looked at the dates of his service . . . he must have been in Desert Storm, the first Gulf War.

Or had something happened to him after he got back that led to his murder of Claire Seldon?

He called Janey Cahill.

"Hey," she said.

"Hey. Who's that counselor you know at the high school?"

"Marcus Simmons?"

"That's him. Do you have his number?"

"Sure. I'll text it to you. What's up?"

"I'm hoping he knows what happened to one of the psychologists over there."

"Who?"

"Grace Portnoy."

"Oh, yeah, I know Grace. You do, too, don't you?"

"How?"

"She's been there for ages. Didn't you ever talk to her about Jason?"

"Maybe." His older son Jason was a student at Ferndale High, but he dropped out after the accident that killed his mother. "I don't remember Jason having anything to do with her. She's still there?"

"Sure," Janey said. "She's terrific."

"Can you help me get in touch with her? I want to ask her about one of my cases."

"Hang on, I'll find the number."

After a few moments, she came back on the line. He wrote down Grace Portnoy's number and said, "Thanks."

"Summer school's still in session, so there's a good chance you'll find her. Tell her hi from me."

"Will do," he said. Then, after a pause, he said, "Doing okay?"

"Yeah," she said. Tentative, not very persuasive. "You?"

"Same. How's your day going?"

"Busy. Still sweeping up after the weekend, as usual."

Janey Cahill was the Ferndale PD youth detective and much of her work came following disastrous weekends for her charges.

"I don't have time right now, but Martin, we should talk."

"Yeah."

"But not now."

"No," he agreed. "Not now."

They disconnected. Even though "we should talk" was always an ominous beginning to a conversation, he felt better after speaking with her. Even though the call didn't last for more than two minutes. Longtime work colleagues, they had been contemplating getting involved with each other now that she was separated from her husband. The problem was, her husband still lived in their basement. She and Preuss had been having more or less serious conversations about how to proceed from here until they decided to put things on pause till her home situation became clearer.

He didn't remember relationships being this hard when he was young. Maybe a function of getting older was realizing just how messy these connections could be. And always were.

He tried the number for Grace Portnoy, and left a message for her when her voicemail came on. He spent another few hours examining the Douglas trial materials and typed up more notes. He closed up the office for the night and went off to see his son.

That relationship, at least, was happily free of complications. He loved Toby, Toby loved him. End of story.

11

Huntington Woods was a suburb just across Eleven Mile Road from Berkley, where his son's group home was, so the staff pushed residents' wheelchairs down a few blocks to the pocket park across from the Huntington Woods Library. Preuss pushed Toby. An aide and a respiratory therapist stayed behind to care for the two residents of the group home who were tethered to ventilators and couldn't make this field trip.

Tonight's entertainment was a trio of thirty-somethings who played a mix of bluegrass and folk and spent their time between songs bantering among themselves, exchanging private jokes that made Preuss feel like he was eavesdropping on a private conversation. But they played decent music. A burly young man played deft guitar, a young woman in short shorts was a great fiddler, and a taciturn bassist played with great flair in what Preuss thought of as the Taliban look—hair shorn down to stubble and a full bristly brown beard.

Preuss sat on the grass next to Toby's wheelchair. Toby was having a wonderful time, as he always did when he listened to music. (Indeed, as he did everywhere, Preuss reflected.) He attended to every note and phrase, laughing and squealing and, when Preuss told him he had to listen quietly, quieting down until his pleasure got the best of him again, and he had to express it vocally.

Preuss's presence added to the boy's pleasure. And certainly to his own. There was no better sound than his son's laughter, and Toby was never sparing with it. The other young people from Toby's home weren't enjoying it as well; Katey seemed to have fallen asleep, and Charley, who was the oldest of the residents and suffered from a degenerative neurological disease, was his usual cranky and disputatious self, insulting the aide who was trying to quiet him down and being generally obnoxious.

The group played for an hour, and after forty-five minutes a few people in the crowd began to quietly pack up and leave. The fiddler said they were going to play three more songs, and they ended with a lively "Foggy Mountain Breakdown." The guitarist played a terrific flat pick version of Earl Scruggs's banjo part that Preuss had never heard before.

He helped get all the group home residents and equipment together, and pushed Toby back to the house. There he gave his son a bath. From his bath chair in the tub, Toby looked up at his father and vocalized something that modulated from a baritone up to a falsetto and back down to baritone again. Preuss leaned down to Toby's eye level and they connected, eyeball to eyeball. Preuss could feel the love passing between them like a current of electricity.

After he got Toby dried off, sitting on the bed with his arm around his son—pink and fragrant as an apple in his pajamas, easing into sleep—Preuss talked about his latest case. With his cerebral palsy, Toby couldn't sit up unsupported, so Preuss had to prop him up.

Preuss told his son what had happened to Jessie Douglas, and Toby hummed a sad and appropriate sound. Toby attended carefully as Preuss talked about the Seldon family, describing for his son the strange weather of the climate in that fractured family.

The veteran of a fractured family himself, Toby listened quietly. Preuss interpreted the boy's silence as the proper compassionate response.

At home in Ferndale, Preuss went around the first floor and turned all the lights on. He wasn't afraid of the dark, but he liked to have the corners lit at night; it made the house seem less cavernous and empty.

He didn't think he could stand another cup of coffee, even decaf—already his mouth felt grainy from the caffeine he had consumed during the day—so he drank a glassful of cold water at the sink and wandered into the living room. He found a CD by Eva Cassidy, the posthumous *Songbird*, and put it on.

He didn't have air conditioning—the heating was a steam boiler with radiators, and it would cost thousands to add ductwork—so the warmth of the day hung close and heavy in the air. Sweating, he stretched out on the sofa and let his thoughts drift.

As he listened to Eva Cassidy's cover of "Autumn Leaves," the aching melancholy of the song made him realize that Ray Douglas's murder of Claire Seldon had the same effect on Jessie Douglas's life as it had on Mary Seldon's. What had brother Larry said about Mary? She went off the deep end after her mother's death . . . Jessie Douglas was no more successful than Mary in getting her life together when her father went to prison.

And now she would never have the chance. Another life ruined by a senseless act of violence.

Linking Mary and Jessie in his mind made him realize Jessie's death must be connected to Claire Seldon's. It was not realistic to think otherwise, even if there was no evidence of the connection yet.

The thought of young lives ruined made him also think about his older son, Jason, out of touch now for several years. Jason had disappeared after his release from the hospital where he recovered from injuries he sustained in the accident that killed his mother when a drunk driver slammed into the car Jeanette and the boys were riding in. Jason blamed his father for causing the circumstances that led to the accident; they were on their way up to Jeanette's mother in Traverse City after Jeanette and Preuss had a monster fight. Swearing it was the end, she couldn't take it anymore, Jeanette put the two boys in the van and headed up north late one night. She told Preuss she was leaving him for good.

As it turned out, she was right. She never made it to her mother's. She was killed instantly in the crash. Toby, in the back seat, propped up and surrounded by pillows, survived with only bruises and cuts, but Jason in the front had a serious closed head injury.

For the first few years after he left, Jason contacted Preuss whenever he needed money, every few months. Lately, though, Jason had gone quiet. Preuss kept tabs on him through police contacts he had developed across the country when Jason would be picked up periodically for panhandling and loitering. But he hadn't heard anything about his older son for the past six months.

Preuss assumed Jason would circle back into his and Toby's orbit when he was ready.

In the meantime, he had Toby . . . sweet, beautiful, frail, profoundly handicapped Toby. Preuss didn't know anyone who loved his life, and the people in it, as much as Toby did. Whenever Preuss took his son anywhere, like the concert tonight, Toby always had the best time of anyone. Of all the lessons he could learn from his son—including the virtues of patience and acceptance—Preuss most wished he could learn to find joy in every moment, as Toby did.

Preuss listened to the rest of the tracks on the CD, concluding with a phenomenal elegiac version of "Somewhere Over the Rainbow." The message of which version, he decided in his present dark state, in the aftermath of the sour taste of too much coffee and too many Seldons, was basically, Don't Hold Your Breath, Pal.

Good advice, thought Martin Preuss. Not one that Toby would agree with, but good all the same.

He went around the house turning out the lights, and climbed the stairs to bed.

Wednesday, July 18, 2012

12

In the morning, after stopping by Toby's house to kiss his son and help get him up and ready for his school day, Preuss sat in his office and punched in the number for Grace Portnoy.

She picked up after two rings. "Dr. Portnoy." A crisp voice, all business. Whatever you're thinking about trying, don't do it, her tone cautioned.

He introduced himself. "I'm an investigator looking into Raymond Douglas's case. You were called as a witness for Raymond's defense at his trial. Do you remember that? It would've been in the early 1990s."

"How could I forget? But Mr. Preuss, I've heard of you. Aren't you with the Ferndale Police?"

"I was. I retired last year. If you have time, Dr. Portnoy, I'd like to speak with you about Raymond."

"How's he doing? Have you seen him lately?"

"Unfortunately, he died in prison not long ago."

"Oh my." Big sigh on the other end of the phone. "So sorry to hear that. That poor man."

"Do you have a few minutes to talk about him?"

"Not sure what I can tell you, after all this time. But I'm happy to help. I have some tests to give this morning, but I can see you at 10:30. Does that work?"

"Perfect. See you then."

During the first part of the morning, he composed the report on his investigation into his restaurant embezzlement case. The assistant manager had been syphoning off $25,000 in proceeds over the past year, and the case was ready to turn over to the police if the restaurant owner wanted that to happen; in Preuss's experience, businesses sometimes didn't want to press charges because of the adverse publicity. He laid out the options for the owner to decide what she wanted to do.

He saved the report to the file, and then it was time to start out for the high school on Pinecrest.

Dr. Grace Portnoy looked to be in her sixties, a trim woman with curly white hair and oversized glasses. She came out to meet Preuss in the Ferndale High School lobby and led him back through a warren of administrative cubicles to her office.

"People think a school psychologist is basically a counselor," she told him as they settled themselves at the round conference table that took up most of her office. "But we do other things entirely."

She had a two-inch-thick manila folder on the table, and pulled it toward her as she spoke. "These are my files for Raymond Douglas." She opened the folder and withdrew several bundles clipped together. "I had to go down to Storage to find them."

She fanned them out in front of her like great playing cards.

"Family-related visits and evaluations," she said as she held a hand over the different piles. "I identified Raymond as learning disabled and socially at-risk, so this is the IEP we developed. Individualized Educational Program," she explained. "Know what they are?"

Rather than mention the dozen IEP meetings he had taken part in for Toby, he simply nodded.

"Reports of collaborations with his teachers. His test scores on the cognitive battery to determine his intellectual functioning and academic potential. Personality assessments to evaluate his levels of emotional and behavioral functioning. The various interventions we tried with him—social skills training, organizational skill building, an overall plan to help him to become more successful . . . Believe me when I say, Mr. Preuss, we tried everything with Raymond."

"Did any of it work?"

"Up to a point. It helped us understand him better. It helped us improve his school-based support system. It may even have helped

Raymond understand himself better. But did it help him succeed academically? Or dispel his demons?" She shook her head sadly. "I wish I could say it did. He kept getting in trouble despite all our efforts. Truancy, fights, failing classes . . ."

"He never graduated, did he?"

She shook her head and rustled through one of the piles. "He left after the eleventh grade. Here." She pulled a paper out of the pile. "His transcript." She handed it across her desk. "All Ds and Es until he dropped out. I heard he joined the army after he left us. He was underage. Must have forged his mother's name."

"Why do you say that?"

"Ever meet her?"

He shook his head. "I never met him, either."

"She was an alcoholic. I don't use that term lightly. Every time I'd have an appointment with her, she showed up stinking of booze—when she even bothered to dry out long enough to get here. When I'd call the house and talk with her, she was barely coherent. The father took off when Raymond was a toddler, so he was really at risk all around. I'm usually not so judgmental about my kids' parents. You never know what troubles people have in their lives. But this woman."

She sighed. "The way she treated that child was criminal. I filed a report with Child Protective Services about it, but they didn't find enough to remove him from the home when they investigated."

"Sounds like a very troubled kid."

"He was," she said. "He was a magnet for trouble. And he spread it where ever he went. Not that his cronies were any angels."

She swiveled in her chair and opened a cupboard behind her. She rapidly swept her hand over three shelves of bound books and withdrew one. "Raymond's yearbook from when he was in the eleventh grade." She opened it to a homeroom page and showed the group photo to Preuss. "That's him."

She tapped a nail on a photo of a kid who looked right into the camera. He was a handsome young man, with dark eyes in an oval face under curly black hair. He looked out blankly, as though already practicing for his mug shots, Preuss thought.

He handed the book back to Dr. Portnoy. She gazed at the teenager's face for a long few moments. "It's always so moving, you know. You look at the faces of these kids, these infants, and think about what life has in store for them. Over the years, I've developed a sixth sense about who's going to stay in trouble and who's going to straighten out. He's one I was wrong about. I had the hubris to think I could save him, or at least nudge him in the right direction. But no."

"Dr. Portnoy," Preuss said, "there's one thing I don't understand. I read the transcripts of Raymond Douglas's murder trial, and you appeared as a character witness for the defense."

"Correct."

"You had only good things to say about him. Yet now you're telling me he was always in trouble?"

"I don't want to give you the wrong impression. He always was basically a good kid. I'm sure you heard that two or three thousand times when you were with the police. But Ray was. When I first met him, when he started the ninth grade, he was wild, sure, but he seemed like he genuinely wanted to get himself squared away."

"So what happened?"

"Two things. First," she said, holding up one finger gnarled with arthritis, "his family. His mother got worse and worse after his little brother died."

"How did he die?"

"Hit by a car on his bicycle. A car ran a stop sign near their house and knocked Brian twenty feet in the air. He was dead by the time he hit the ground. Raymond had just started the tenth grade. He adored his little brother, and I think that was the thing that really knocked him off the rails. And the second thing was, he fell in with a crowd that egged him on, encouraging him to act out."

Dr. Portnoy closed the yearbook. "The tenth grade was really his downfall. That's when he started hanging out with a group of wild ones. The ringleader was a boy named Eugene Washburn. They were all in the same homeroom. You've heard of Washburn Buick on Woodward?"

Preuss nodded.

"That was Eugene's father. I hear Eugene's running the place now. But oh, he was a hellion in his time, that boy. All the others straightened themselves out once Raymond left school. They all went on to college and good lives, good careers. They come back at career nights to visit, sometimes. But Raymond never could shake his past.

"So no, Mr. Preuss, I had no problems talking about his promise and his intelligence, and his essentially good character, because I believed it all. And he didn't have many others on his side back then. Who knows what other mental or emotional problems started manifesting after he left school? And then, of course, he joined the army, and they turned him into a killer."

She raised her hands as though to stop herself. "Don't get me started on that. Too many kids around here still think the army's their only option. The long and short of it is, Ray Douglas was a troubled young man when he left us, and a real mess when he came home from the war. And I guess you know the rest."

"Do you know if he was in touch with his old gang once he got home from the army?"

"No idea," she said. "Sorry. You'd have to ask them."

"Is there any other family you know about? Or any friends or associates?"

"Not to my knowledge. Mother's dead, and what kind of friends he might have is anybody's guess."

He said he wouldn't take up any more of her time. He decided not to tell her about Ray's daughter; she seemed distraught enough about how Ray turned out. "I appreciate what you've told me."

When he returned to his Explorer, his phone was buzzing with a new call.

Mary Seldon.

13

"*That's* what that woman told you? My mother's death was 'a great blow' to my father?"

Mary Seldon twisted her face in what may have been a smile in the bright morning sunshine. She had been walking Button in the park across from her condo when Preuss drove up.

"What's your version?" he asked.

"Whatever other effects it had on him," she said, "I can guarantee you it wasn't 'a great blow.'"

She watched her little dog stop, sniff around, and leave a small brown turd near the swing set. Mary handed the leash to Preuss and bent to scoop up the dropping in a plastic bag she wore over her hand. She pulled the bag inside out and tied it at the neck. Her hand trembled, but she had the movement down.

She dropped the bag off in a trash can, and Preuss felt the gentle tug of the animal against the leash. He thought again about getting a dog.

Mary returned to take Button's leash back and led them to a park bench, where they sat.

"I was mulling over what we talked about yesterday," she said. "I thought it would be a good thing for me to talk it through. The death of my mother, that is."

"I appreciate the call."

"You asked me how my father took her murder?"

He nodded for her to continue.

She paused to gather her thoughts, then said, "We'd just gotten back from the cemetery, and I found him sitting alone in their bedroom. On their bed. I thought the reality of what happened was finally sinking in. He hadn't shown much reaction since her body was found. Very stoic, you know. Manly. So I tiptoed in and sat beside him. I thought we were going to reminisce or something. Or at least share our grief in some way. But he picked up his head and looked at me, and you know what he said?"

Preuss shook his head.

"He said, 'Honey, I hope you don't expect me to be alone for the rest of my life, because I just can't do it. I don't plan to be alone for very long.'"

She lit a cigarette with a savage anger, as though the conversation had just happened and she was still boiling.

"Nothing about my mother, nothing about me or the boys, nothing about the family and what we'd lost. Just himself, and his plan to not be alone."

Preuss said nothing.

"The dirt hadn't even settled on her grave, and there he was, already talking about moving on."

"Must have been hard to hear that," he agreed.

"That woman told you they were married a year after my mother died? It was more like six months. Six months, can you believe it? He didn't even make a show of being in mourning. That sound like 'a great blow' to you?"

She jerked Button away from an empty soda can on the ground. "Sweetie, that's dirty," she said.

"How about the story of how they met? Through a mutual friend? Was that true?"

"As far as I know."

"Did you know the friend?"

"He was an old buddy of my father's. My godfather, as it happens. His second wife was a business associate of Christine's. Christine was an event planner for chichi galas, or some such thing. So my father and his friend both wound up with their trophy wives."

Preuss considered that. "Do you have his number? I'd like to speak with him."

"I might. Back at the condo. What good would that do? He didn't even know the guy who killed my mother."

"Maybe not," Preuss said, "but he may have other information. I'm trying to talk to everybody involved with this. Plus, I'm interested in the discrepancy between Christine's version and yours. She said they were married a year after your mother died, but you say it was six months."

"You think I'm lying?"

"Not at all."

"It was six months, almost to the day. She says otherwise, she's the liar, not me. Button, are you finished?"

The dog looked up at his mistress. Button's soulful brown eyes were partly obscured by tufts of coarse hair. He snorted and pulled at the leash in the direction of the way home.

"Guess so," Mary said, and let the little dog, straining and gasping at the collar, lead the way back across the street.

Inside her condo, she searched until she found the name and phone number of the friend who had introduced her father to his second wife, then copied the information onto a Post-it Note. Preuss thanked her and pocketed the paper. "It sounds like you don't care much for your stepmother," he said.

"Picked up on that, did you? You *are* a good detective."

He let that go by, writing it off to her anger and sadness at reliving this episode. "Did she do something else to you? Besides marry your father, that is."

"I don't have anything against her for marrying my father. He was a great catch—he's handsome, he's loaded—a wealthy widower, who wouldn't go for him?"

She flicked her hair out of her face. "Thing is, she's a gold-digger. She saw a lonely, wealthy man and she went after him. And he fell hard for her. I can't stand the woman. The real problem was," she said, then stopped. She seemed to struggle with what she was about to say.

"Was what?"

Mary seemed to be debating with herself whether to say something further.

"Was what?" he asked again.

"When I was having my issues—the ones I told you about?"

He nodded.

"She had no sympathy for me. I begged my father to help me, but she totally turned him against me. I asked for money, sure, but I also asked if I could stay with him for a while, just to get myself out of the environment I was in. I knew if I was going to have a chance, I had to get away from the people around me. My brothers both had families, I couldn't ask them. She said absolutely not. Wouldn't even let me stay overnight one of the times when I got out of rehab and had no place else to go. And he went along with it."

She lit another cigarette, blew the smoke out of the side of her mouth away from Preuss.

"I never felt like he loved me," she said. "The boys were the apple of his eye, not me. They would have done anything for him. I was just 'the girl.' Always closer to my mother.

"But shit, he was my father," she continued. "And that woman completely turned him against me. *That's* what I hold against her, Mr. Preuss."

Mary Seldon had given him the name Oliver Price. The number was a 212 area code, Manhattan.

After three rings, Preuss was getting ready to leave a message when a woman's voice answered by repeating the number.

"I'm calling for Oliver Price," he said. "Is this the correct number?"

"This is Mrs. Price," the woman said. She sounded younger than he expected, but he remembered what Mary Seldon had said about her father and his best friend marrying trophy wives. If that was true, she would be younger.

"Is your husband—"

"My husband passed away," she interrupted.

"Oh. I'm sorry to hear that."

"Thank you. Five years this coming Christmas. He had a heart attack. Well, a series of heart attacks. The last one did him in."

"My condolences."

"Thank you," she said again.

"You and your husband were friends of William Seldon, I understand."

"Yes. My husband, especially. They were roommates in college. U of M."

He explained who he was. "I'm doing some background work on the family, and I was given your number by William's daughter Mary."

That put her on her guard. "Mary," she said frostily. He could sense her mouth twisted in disapproval. "You've spoken with her?"

"I have."

"How is she?"

"She seems to be doing well."

In the short pause that followed, Preuss thought he might have sensed a frisson of disappointment from the woman at this news.

"What's she doing with herself nowadays?" she asked.

That question could be taken a number of different ways. Preuss decided to sidestep it entirely. "Mrs. Price," he said, "Mary gave me your husband's name as the one who introduced William and Christine."

"I'm the one who did that, actually," she said. "Christine was my friend."

"How did you get them together?"

"Oh," she said, and laughed, a high tinkle of remembrance, "it was at one of our parties. Whenever Bill came to town on business, we threw him a party. We threw the most marvelous parties, my husband and I." *Maah-velous paah-ties.*

"And Christine was at one of them?"

"She was at most of them. She was a real live wire, just so full of life. And she and Bill hit it off right away. Just like they were made for each other."

I'll bet they did, Preuss thought.

"Mrs. Price, about how long would you say Christine and William have known each other?"

"Well, let's see," the woman said. "Bill came to town two or three times a year for business . . ."

"And every time he came, you had a party for him."

"Yes."

"And at every party Christine was there?"

"Most every one."

"So it sounds like they'd known each other for years. Even before Claire died."

"Yes. Christine used to come with her husband, and then when he passed away she kept coming solo."

"When did her husband die?"

He heard her expel a breath on the other end of the phone line. "It must have been sometime in the late eighties."

Years before Claire died, Preuss thought.

"Did Claire Seldon also come to these parties?" he asked.

"Bill hardly ever brought Claire to New York with him. Not that I blamed him, frankly. The few times I met her, I found her to be somewhat of a cold fish. Whenever we were all four of us together, she always had this sort of sour look on her face, like she wished she could be anyplace else but where we were. It was terrible when she was killed, don't get me wrong. I hate to speak ill of the dead."

"How much did you know about her murder?"

"Not much at all. Really, just that Bill was completely devastated. My Oliver flew right to Michigan as soon as he heard about it. And Christine stepped right up, too. With all her *joie de vivre*, she was just what Bill needed."

"Have you kept in touch with them?"

"Not as often as I'd like," she said. "Once Bill retired, they didn't come to town as often."

"Isn't that odd? I would have thought with more leisure, they'd travel to New York more often."

"Just didn't work out that way, I guess."

He thanked her and told her he wouldn't take up any more of her time.

"No problem," Betty Price sang. "Always happy to chat about friends. And if you see Chrissy and Bill, say hello to them for me, won't you?"

"I'll make sure I do," Preuss said.

14

He drove back to the office and recorded the notes of his conversations with Dr. Portnoy, Mary Seldon, and Betty Price. According to Mary and Christine Seldon, William Seldon met his future wife only after his first wife had died. Yet Betty Price said he had known Christine for years prior to Claire's death in 1992.

And Claire Seldon hardly ever came to New York with her husband. That would have given him the time and space he needed to spend time with the joyous and vivacious Christine, without anyone in Michigan knowing.

Let's suppose something was going on between the two of them, Preuss thought, long before they told everyone they met for the first time.

Let's say, furthermore, that Seldon decided he wanted to be free to marry Christine. Would that be enough of a motive for arranging his wife's murder? Why not just divorce her? Why take the incredibly risky—not to say insane—step of organizing her murder?

And how would he have gotten in touch with a deranged war vet to get it done? Especially when the vet was pursuing his own delusion about becoming chief of police?

If, as he intuited the night before, Claire Seldon's death was connected with Jessie Douglas's, then he needed to know how Reg Trombley was making out with Jessie's case.

Preuss called him.

Trombley picked up right away.

"It's Martin. Had lunch yet?"

Preuss suggested they meet at Rosie O'Grady's, a sports bar in Ferndale with television monitors in every sightline, including one at every table, so no sports score anywhere in the world would go unnoticed. When Trombley balked, Preuss remembered it might not be a good idea for them to be seen together in Ferndale, so Preuss suggested a restaurant out on Telegraph and Fifteen Mile, in Bloomfield Hills.

After they ordered their food, Trombley said, "Up until this morning, the investigation was starting to focus on the boyfriend. Guy name of Richard Ouellette. Ring a bell?"

"No."

"Lives out near Milan."

"Why are you looking at him?"

"His record, for one thing. He did time for assaulting his ex-wife a while back. He used to beat her, but she never pressed charges until the last time, when he gave her a concussion and broken jaw."

"You closed in on him fast."

"We doze, but we never close, my brother. Besides, what did you used to say? It's always the boyfriend?"

"I used to say it's always the uncle, but I was talking about something else."

"I always keep your little pearls in mind. Anyway, I went out to Milan myself early today and saw him at his house."

"Nice work."

"Here's the bad news. He's got a solid alibi for Sunday night and Monday morning."

"Which is?"

"He's a maintenance man at Schultz Bottled Gas out there. He usually works the afternoon shift, three to eleven, but on Sunday he said he worked a double. He was at the plant from three on Sunday afternoon until seven o'clock Monday morning."

"And Jessie Douglas was killed sometime Sunday night."

"Still waiting for the medical examiner's report, but the coroner said she thought that's when it was. I checked with Ouellette's supervisor, and he accounted for his movements the whole time."

"He didn't have any breaks?"

"Nothing with enough time to drive all the way into Ferndale and back. They had a plumbing problem out there, pipes breaking and so forth, and they kept him on to help with the cleanup. He went on breaks, but the supervisor says Ouellette was never out of his sight for more than twenty minutes at a time. That wouldn't have given him enough time to get down here, do the deed, and get back to Milan."

"No," Preuss agreed.

"So it's not the boyfriend."

"Does he have it in for her? Does anybody?"

"Not that we can tell. Nobody knows much about her. On the way back from Milan, I stopped off at the trailer park where she lived. Dusty little hole in the ground in Saline. I spoke with the trailer park manager, but there wasn't anything she could tell me."

"Text me her address," Preuss said. "You don't mind, I might take a run out there and look around."

"I'll do it now."

Trombley opened his notepad and texted the address.

"It's the smallish trailer in the northwest corner of the park," he said. "Brown and cream, rundown. Spare key's under the fake frog in the front yard."

"Thanks."

"Her work history's spotty, mostly jobs in service industries— waitressing, motel housekeeping, like that—and temp gigs like the one she had at the fair. That's how she met Ouellette . . . a temp job in housekeeping at the gas plant."

"How'd she get those?"

"She registered with temp agencies here and across the country. She's done a lot of drifting. Collected some charges for minor offenses here and there around the country, drunk and disorderly type things. She started college at Western Michigan, but left during her first year. From then on, seems like she lived on the margins. Always wound up coming back here, though."

"Have you spoken with the Seldons?"

"Oh yeah."

"Bunch of charmers, right?"

"No kidding. Thing is, the family has an alibi for Sunday night. The wife, Christine, threw a dinner party for William Seldon's birthday, and both brothers and their families were there, plus some guests. Didn't break up till after midnight. I have the guest list but haven't had a chance to work my way through all the names yet. Otherwise, I'm still trying to piece together Jessica's movements on her last day. She used a burner for a cell phone so we can't do a phone dump."

"Nobody saw her after the street fair closed?"

"The manager of the Bushmills tent said they closed up at eight when the fair ended, then took another hour to clean up and break down the tent and load up their truck. Then he told her she could take off. He paid her, and she walked away into the night."

"He didn't see where she went?"

"Only thing we know about is the call she made to you just after nine."

Preuss considered that.

"There's a 2007 Chevy Cruze registered in her name," Trombley said. "We found it up on East Cambourne. Arnie Biederman and the Evidence Tech guys are going over it."

"You saw her body?"

"I did. Pretty banged up. Don't know if that was from a beating or was post-mortem from the dumpster. M.E.'ll let us know. Arnie's going to go over the scene, and he'll let me know what kind of forensics he finds."

"In a dumpster? After a street fair? Good luck with that."

Trombley shrugged. "Anything there, Arnie'll find it."

Preuss said, "The boyfriend seemed too easy."

"The vast majority of murdered women are killed by lovers or husbands," Trombley pointed out.

"I know. But still."

"Most of these guys aren't criminal masterminds, you know. You taught me that. Fact she was dumped near where she'd last been seen suggested a crime of opportunity. Probably wasn't terribly well thought-through. Possibly a random crime."

They ate in silence for a few minutes. Then Preuss caught Trombley up on the conversations he'd been having.

"I'm going to talk with a friend of the first Mrs. Seldon later on today," Preuss said. "I don't have as much of an impression of her as I'd like. I'm hoping the friend can fill in."

"Sounds good," Trombley agreed.

"You know," Preuss said, "when I spoke with her on the phone on Sunday night, Jessie told me she'd found out something. I'm wondering if she'd been getting too close to whoever it was who helped her father all those years ago."

"If such a person exists."

"Right. There's that."

"Who else knew she was asking about it?"

Preuss thought for a moment. "Shelley Larkin, for one. The reporter."

"Jessica might have also said something to the boyfriend, Ouellette," Trombley suggested. "He didn't mention it, but then again, I didn't ask him. I'll run that down with him."

"Shelley told me Jessie'd been trying to shop her story to the news media around town, but nobody bit except Shelley. So who knows how many other people she told?"

"Might be no way of knowing."

"No," Preuss agreed.

Then he had a distressing thought.

Before he could speak it, Trombley said, "Think she might have told your little reporter friend who she talked with? Worth a conversation with her."

"Reg," Preuss said, "you took the words right out of my mouth."

15

Preuss put the call through to Shelley Larkin. In contrast to the way
he felt a few years ago, he did not particularly want to speak with her
now. But Trombley was right, and he had the same thought a second
before Trombley opened his mouth: Shelley might know the names of
the people Jessie Douglas had tried to sell on her story. And there
might be some way to find a connection to whoever killed her.

It was the longest of shots, but it was one of the few directions
open to them right now.

Shelley told him she had only a small window to see him between appointments. She said she was working on a story comparing
the election campaigns of Mitt Romney and Barack Obama in Michigan that summer, and she had a full calendar of interviews for the
rest of the day and evening.

The *Metro Voice* offices were on Woodward Heights Boulevard in Ferndale, in a long, low building in an area where light industry abutted a
residential section. Shelley came out to meet him in the lobby, and
took his arm and walked him outside to the sprawling parking lot.
With her ascension into the ranks of full-time reporters, she had
bumped up her wardrobe to a better grade of tee shirt and Levis.

"Let's walk," she said. She led him across Woodward Heights
and down a side street with a mix of older bungalows on one side of
the street and newer apartment units with the high-tech look of stain-
less-steel microwave ovens on the other.

"Afraid to be seen with me?" he asked.

"No," she said. "I just needed to get out for a while. Clear my head."

"Pretty big story you're working on."

"I *know*! I've been wanting to get more into politics. Now I'm on staff, I have a better shot at it than when I was a stringer."

"That reminds me," Preuss said. "This conversation is all off the record, right?"

She gave his arm a playful slap. "Do you have to ask?"

"That's not really a denial."

"It's off the record. Satisfied?"

"Just want to get that straight."

They strolled in silence for a few moments, then she said, "So what's up?"

"When you talked with Jessie, did she tell you who she pitched her story to?"

She thought about that. "She told me she approached all the TV stations, and called the *News* and the *Free Press* before she got to us."

"She mention any names?"

"She said she got zero interest from the papers, but didn't mention anybody in particular. I assume she spoke with the Features desk editors. She did say a couple TV people seemed like they might be interested. Pretty sure she told me it was Brad Donahue from Channel 7 and Carrie Kaye from Channel 4. Hang on, I was taking notes as we talked. Got them here."

She opened a file on her phone. "Yeah, those were the two. Donahue and Kaye."

"Anything come of either one?"

"I think they were the only ones who called her back. Neither one wanted to follow up. And nobody else did, either. That's how come she worked her way down the food chain to me. Why's this important?"

"I'm trying to get a sense of who else might have known what she was doing."

"Think that has something to do with what happened to her?"

"Can't rule it out."

"You're sounding very like a police detective again."

"Why is that surprising?"

"It's not," she said, smiling.

That tooth.

He had the sudden thought that she knew exactly what its effect on him was. And used it strategically.

"I'm not criticizing," she said.

"Have you told anyone?"

"Not yet. I wanted to flesh it out a bit more. My editor knows, but he didn't think much of it. You're the only one I've told. And I haven't heard anything more since the last time we talked. Though honestly, I've been distracted by this other story. It's going to be a *big* one for me. Maybe even a cover."

They walked along in silence till they came to the end of the block.

"We should start back," she said.

They began retracing their steps toward the newspaper building.

"Martin," she said, her forehead wrinkled in thought. "I was glad you called. I'd like to see you again."

"'Again'? Remind me when we actually saw each other?"

She smiled. "Things were a little up in the air back then."

"A little."

"What do you think?"

They walked along in silence for a few paces. "It seems to me," Preuss said, "there was also some confusion on my part about the nature of your sexuality."

She said nothing.

"Or was I wrong?"

"No," she said, "you weren't wrong. Confusion on my part, too."

"Any less confused?"

"It's just that seeing you again made me remember how much I enjoyed the time we spent together."

"Which doesn't exactly answer the question," he said.

When she made no reply, he said, "So now you've decided you want to see me, and what, I'm supposed to drop everything because you're ready?"

"No," she said, her defensive tone indicating she picked up on his sudden and poorly-disguised irritation. But she didn't offer an alternative interpretation.

Then she said, "I'm deeply sorry. About before, I mean. I really am."

"Ancient history."

They stopped at the corner of Woodward Heights to let a few cars go by, then crossed back to the *Metro Voice* building.

"So?" she said. "Give it another try?"

He walked her to the front door, then paused. "Let me think about it, okay?"

She held his eyes for another few seconds, then glanced at the time on the phone she had been holding in her hand.

"I gotta get back in," she said.

"Thanks for what you told me."

She flicked her head as though clearing her wavy hair back from her face, even though it wasn't in her eyes. Then she raised a hand in farewell and headed toward the building entrance.

Back in the Explorer, he wrote down the names of the two journalists she mentioned. He sat gazing at the front door of the building, remembering a time a few years ago when he would have loved to have had that conversation with her. Then he searched his phone for the numbers for the Channel 7 and Channel 4 news rooms.

Carrie Kaye wasn't available, but Brad Donahue was.

"I'm just on my way out the door," Donahue said. His voice had the forced, deep, loud, and rushed quality of a Very Important Media Guy. "What's this about?"

"I'd rather talk to you in person," Preuss said.

"Where are you now?"

"Ferndale."

"I'm on my way out to some kind of political demo in Southfield. Can you meet me there? I've got to grab some stand-ups, but it shouldn't take long. We can talk while my cameraman gets the visuals."

"I can do that."

"Know where the Southfield Civic Center is?"

"I think I can find it," said Martin Preuss dryly, and disconnected.

What Brad Donahue thought was a political demonstration was actually a protest against increases in property taxes in Southfield. Preuss parked in the lot outside the Southfield Police Department and walked past the building to an outdoor courtyard in front of the Southfield Pavilion.

This was as close as the protesters could get to the Building Assessor's offices. About a hundred people, mostly older adults, marched around the courtyard holding signs decrying the recent tax hike and shouting, "Hey Hey, Ho Ho, We Don't Want to Pay No Mo'!" as they marched. A handful of Southfield police officers stood by, but the marchers were orderly if noisy.

Donahue was off to the side, interviewing a woman while his cameraman recorded the interview from different angles. Donahue was tall and slick, with an impeccably tailored brown suit. He inclined his head sympathetically as he held the microphone in front of his subject. When he was in the Ferndale PD, Preuss had had a few dealings with Donahue; he was mostly accurate in his reporting, though he was grating in his self-regard.

Donahue wrapped the interview and held a quick conference with his cameraman, who hefted his ENG camera and wandered among the picketers, shooting random scenes.

Preuss came up and introduced himself. "We just talked on the phone," he said.

"Right right right." Donahue looked closely at Preuss. "Have we met before?"

Preuss nodded. "I used to be with the Ferndale police."

"Knew it. Never forget a face. What are you doing now?"

"Private investigation," Preuss said.

"Oh yeah? Private dick?"

"Did you speak with a woman named Jessie Douglas?"

"Is she one of your cases?"

"Did you speak with her, sir?"

Donahue blew out his cheeks. "Name doesn't ring a bell." He began wrapping up his microphone cord. "What's she done?"

"She's the daughter of Raymond Douglas," Preuss said. "He went to prison for a local kidnapping-murder about twenty years ago. Jessie was looking for someone to listen to her story about her father having an accomplice."

"Oh, right right right," Donahue said. "I do remember. Nice girl. Sad story. I listened, but I had to tell her no. Might be a good human interest piece for the print media, but for us, uh-uh. I just didn't see the possibility for good visuals. That's what's important in TV. If I can't see it, it's no good to me."

"Did you tell anybody what she asked about? Your news director, maybe? One of your colleagues at the station?"

Donahue shook his head. "I didn't need to check with my director. I knew what he'd say."

"And you didn't mention it to anyone else?"

Donahue gave him a pitying half-smile. "Do you know how many times a day I get pitched a story? If I brought my news director even a quarter of those, I'd never get anything else done."

"Okay. Thanks."

"That it?"

"That's it." Preuss turned to go.

"Are you working with her?" Donahue asked.

When Preuss didn't answer, Donahue said, "Wait, you're a private eye? You must have a million stories. Hey, wait, come back!"

Preuss raised a hand in farewell and kept going to his car.

He stopped at a Coney Island on Woodward for a container of coffee. He was about to start out in the Explorer when his cell rang.

Carrie Kaye, returning his call, her voice low and as brusque and self-important as Brad Donahue's.

He explained what he wanted and asked if they could meet.

"Impossible," she said. "This is a crazy busy day. I have no time."

"Then I'll be brief. Do you remember speaking with a woman named Jessie Douglas?"

In the background, Preuss heard the sound of a motor that indicated Carrie Kaye was calling from the road. "What's the name again?"

"Jessie Douglas."

Preuss heard her say, "Turn here," an instruction to her driver. Then she said, "Sorry, and you are?"

He swallowed his annoyance at the limits of her attention span and said his own name again.

"No," she said, "I don't recall speaking to her."

"She never called you? Trying to sell you on a story about her father in prison? His name was Raymond Douglas. This would have been sometime in the past week or two."

"No," Carrie Kaye said.

"So you wouldn't have spoken with anyone about her," Preuss said, more a statement than a question. "Or followed up on the story."

"If I don't remember her, I'm not likely to talk about her, am I?" Before he could answer, she said, "Anything else?"

"No. I appreciate your time."

"Thank you for calling Channel 4 News," she said automatically, and disconnected.

So much for the two leads with reporters, he thought.

Time for a road trip.

16

Saline was a small town an hour west of Detroit, past Ypsilanti and below Ann Arbor. Having grown up in Ypsilanti, where his parents were professors—his father of history, his mother of English—Preuss had been to Saline many times as a young man, most often for the annual Celtic Festival.

He had never had occasion, however, to visit the Saline Springs Estates, which was not actually in Saline but outside the town limits. It wasn't much an an estate, either; it was a small, not terribly well-kept-up trailer park, essentially a dusty field with utility hookups where people could park their run-down single- and double-wides.

He immediately picked Jessie Douglas's trailer out of the dozen or so docked around the park. Her father had been in the Ionia Correctional Facility, which was closer to Grand Rapids, on the other side of the state. So what was Jessie doing here?

He parked beside the brown and cream vehicle and walked around the outside. It was a beat-up RV with flat tires that someone had propped up on cinder blocks. It had dents all over, including a large one on the right rear that was starting to rust. The back bumper was wired on.

Preuss looked around the ground beside the van until he saw something that looked like a frog lost in the high grass—a small resin figurine with an enormous mouth. He picked it up, and sure enough found a key on a brass ring pressed into the bottom.

The key fit into the RV's side door lock but turned with difficulty. The lock was stiff and old and going to rust, so he had to work the key back and forth a few times before he got the door opened.

He stepped up into disorganized, cramped quarters and the hot, sour, musty smell of dirty clothes moldering in an enclosed space. To the right was a tiny stove/refrigerator combination, and next to that was a shelf holding a few cans of baked beans and soup, as well as an open box of Cap'n Crunch and boxes of mac and cheese mix. Straight ahead was another cupboard packed with folded clothing, and a tiny toilet and shower. Taking up the left end was a bed covered with a sloppy pile of sheets and tee shirts and piles of underpants that may or may not have been clean.

He gloved up and cranked open the side windows, which let in a breath of cooler air but did nothing for the musty smell. He sorted through the clothes that were strewn over the bed and around the wardrobe, then got down on his hands and knees and searched around the floor for a clue to Jessie Douglas's fate.

He pushed aside the tee shirts and Levis and underthings that comprised her wardrobe. Under the bed were more dirty underpants and tee shirts. He brushed them aside and saw only dust mice.

He searched through the cupboards, then concluded there seemed to be nothing useful here. Except maybe enough to give Preuss a better sense of Jessie Douglas as a lonely, isolated young woman constantly on the move, with no serious connections with anyone, no interests beyond proving something about her father that may or may not be true.

He locked up the RV, replaced the key under the frog statue, and walked back to his car. A woman was leaning against it with her arms folded. She was short and thin as a nail, with wiry red hair going grey and a broad freckled forehead. She looked worn and haggard, as if she were bone-tired of her life.

"Mind telling me what you were doing in there?" she asked, pointing the top of her head toward Jessie's motor home.

He pulled a business card from his wallet and handed it to her. "I'm a private investigator. I'm helping the police with an investigation concerning the young woman who lives there. Jessie Douglas."

She eyed the card with suspicion.

"What kind of investigation?"

It occurred to Preuss she might not know about Jessie. But who was she?

"Sorry," he said, "you are?"

"I manage this park. Still haven't told me what you were doing in there."

"I'm sorry to tell you the woman who lives there was found dead on Monday."

She looked down at his card, then back up at him. "Yeah, there was a black cop out here this morning. Told me about it. Looked around in there, too."

"Detective Trombley, Ferndale Police."

"That was him."

"I'm trying to find something that might point to who killed her."

"Did you? Find anything, I mean?"

"Afraid not," Preuss said. "How well did you know her?"

She lifted a shoulder. "I knew her."

"When was the last time you saw her?"

The woman took a swipe at her nose with a thumb, like a boxer. "Saturday. Day before she died."

"Did you talk to her?"

The woman nodded.

"Did she seem upset about anything? Or say anything you can think of that might seem out of the ordinary?"

She looked at his business card again, then back at him. "Who'd you say you were again?"

"An investigator working with the cop you talked to," he said, though that wasn't strictly true.

She considered Preuss. "You knew this girl?" she asked.

"I met her once, the day she died. We talked again on the phone the same night. She wanted me to help her with something, but I never got the chance. She seemed like a good person. I'd like to find out what happened to her."

"Any ideas so far?"

"The police are following a few lines of inquiry."

"You sound like a cop."

"Used to be."

"Get kicked off the force?"

He shook his head. "Retired. Before they could throw me off."

She looked at his card again. "Lines of inquiry," she said. "But nothing for sure?"

"They're doing the best they can."

She nodded and eyed him again. "But you knew her, you said?"

"I did."

She seemed to decide something. "Come with me."

She led him back to the trailer park office, a small cinder block building by the park entrance. Inside, she said, "Wait there," and pointed to a chair. She went behind the counter and into a back room.

Obediently, he sat. On the Masonite paneled walls were black and white photos of the silver bullets of vintage Airstream trailers.

In a minute she returned and stood on the other side of the counter from Preuss. "Here."

She handed a book across to him. It was a yearbook for Ferndale high school from 1986 . . . the same yearbook Grace Portnoy had showed him.

"Can I ask where you got this?"

"From Jessie," she said. "She asked me to hang onto it."

"When?"

"The morning she died."

"Did she say why?"

She shook her head. "I didn't talk to her. She just left it with this note."

She reached into a drawer of the desk behind the counter and handed him a sheet of paper folded into thirds. He unfolded it and read:

Mom—
Can you keep this for me? Tell you what it's about later. Give
Angie a hug for me.
    Love you,
      J

He looked up at her. "'Mom'?"

She nodded. "Renee Cacavelli."

Two mysteries solved, then . . . why Jessie kept coming back to this area—her mother was here—and whose Visa Jessie had.

"It was your credit card Jessie was using," Preuss said.

She nodded. "She'd show up every so often, usually with some kind of crisis or other. This last time, she was having hard times again. That RV was empty and abandoned, so I let her stay there and use my card for necessities. Least I could do now," she added. "I wasn't much of a mother when she was young."

He handed her back the note, and she returned it to her desk.

"I'm going to have to clean that motor home up and do something with it," Renee said. "I just don't have the heart right now."

"No," Preuss said. "Might be best to leave it alone for now anyway. Sorry for your loss."

She accepted with a grimace that turned to tears filling her eyes. "I told her this was no way for her to live. Not somebody with her potential. But it didn't come to nothing."

"May I borrow this?" He held up the yearbook. "I'll get it back. It might be important."

"If it helps find who killed her."

"Your daughter asked me to look into her father's case. She said he told her somebody helped him with the kidnapping of the woman he killed."

"Yeah. She told me the same thing."

"What did you think about that?"

She considered the question. "Honestly, I haven't been in touch with him, so I couldn't tell you what was going on in his life. Now or ever."

"When was the last time you saw him?"

"When he got home from Iraq."

"Not since?"

"Well, yeah, off and on, until he went to prison. Mostly we talked about Jessie."

"So you wouldn't know any friends Ray might have, or associates who could have helped with the killing of that woman?"

"You got me."

"How about anyone he hung around with?"

She shook her head. "I had problems of my own back then. He knocked me up and went into the army and that was it for him and me. My parents mostly raised Jessie. I wasn't around much for her, either. Guess she takes after me, with all her wandering."

She looked across the RV park to the woods in the distance. "Took after me, I mean. Time I got my head on straight, she was grown."

She looked wistfully at Jessie's RV. "Since she's been back this last time, I've been trying to make up for things I missed with her. You know what they say, right? Better late than . . ."

Her voice trailed off.

She couldn't finish the sentence.

He waited a few moments, then said, "The note said 'Give Angie a hug.' Who's Angie?"

She motioned for him to follow her around the counter and into the back room, which turned out to be set up like a kitchen, with a card table and four chairs in the middle of the room and a sink, stove, and small refrigerator at the edges. Sitting at the card table, coloring a book of circus animals, was a little girl. She might have been four or five, with a round face and a wild head of curly brown hair that trembled as she used an electric blue crayon to attack the drawing of an elephant with a comical, open-mouthed intensity.

She looked up at Preuss, then, finding him uninteresting, returned to her coloring.

"Yours?" Preuss asked Renee.

She shook her head. "Jessie's," she mouthed silently.

Preuss looked back at the girl and searched for a resemblance to Jessie Douglas. He thought he could see similarities in her jaw line and the shape and color of her eyes.

"Angie, hon, you doing okay?" Renee asked.

Without looking up, Angie stopped, considered her artwork with a cocked head, and nodded. She held up the paper for Renee to admire.

"Looks great, sweetie."

Angie gave her a proud smile and returned to her coloring.

Renee led Preuss back outside the office. "She's been staying with me," Renee said. "I've been trying to do for her what I couldn't do for Jessie."

She shook her head sadly. "So much to make up for. Plan was, once Jessie got herself ready to be a full-time mother, I'd let her take Angie. Never gonna happen now."

"Does Angie know about Jessie?"

"No. Not sure how to tell her. Not even sure I believe it myself."

"No father in the picture?"

Renee scoffed. "Angie doesn't even think Jessie's her mother."

He looked back at the child, coloring so contentedly, and thought again about how her mother ended up, covered in garbage in a dumpster. Another lost child growing up in the world. Each generation makes more. There didn't seem to be an end to it.

17

On the way back from Saline, he called Roxanne Stewart, Claire's old friend, to see if this would be too late to see her. She said she could see him, but she and her husband had a function that evening so if he wanted to talk to her today, it couldn't be too late.

She lived in a sprawling brick Tudor house near the Country Club of Detroit in Grosse Pointe Farms. She answered the door in full evening gown getup, complete with pearls and diamond earrings that picked up the late afternoon sun glittering off Lake St. Clair across Jefferson Avenue. If I were that kind of wise-cracking private eye, Preuss thought, I'd tell her how she didn't have to get dressed up for me.

But she beat him to it.

"I don't usually get this dolled up for my visitors," she said. "My husband and I are going to a fundraising party for the MS Society tonight." She stepped aside for him to enter.

"I appreciate your seeing me at such short notice," Preuss said.

She waved it away. "Soon as I heard this was about Claire," she said, "I'd have made time, one way or another. Sit."

She pointed toward a sofa that ran almost the length of the living room. He disappeared into plush beige cushions. She sat on another sofa opposite. She had silver hair swept back from a high forehead and bright blue eyes.

"I'd offer you something," she said, "but I sent our girl home for the day and I don't have anything prepared."

"Not a problem."

"What can I tell you?" she asked. "I was under the impression Claire's killer had been caught and punished."

"He was," Preuss said. He leaned forward to keep from getting swallowed in the cushions. "In fact, he died in prison not long ago."

"Good," she said. "I hope it was a long and painful death."

"I'm investigating the circumstances of Mrs. Seldon's death. Part of that is getting a better sense of her."

Roxanne Stewart took a deep breath, let it out slowly. "I'm sorry to say, she was not a happy woman. I knew her for most of her life. I was probably her closest friend. In her younger days, she was more carefree. Marriage to that man took all the joy out of her."

He remembered Betty Price raving about Christine Seldon's *joie de vivre*. Apparently, Claire had some of that, too. Once.

"In what way?"

She sized him up. "How much do you know about her?"

"Not much. That's what I'm hoping you'll help me with."

She leaned back and gave him Claire's story.

Claire Johnson came from Ferndale, Roxanne said. She and Claire met in elementary school and stayed friends even as their lives took them on different paths.

Claire was the only child of well-off parents. Once his industrial chemical company began to take off, her father, Curtis Johnson, moved the family from Ferndale to Bloomfield Hills. Her parents had a summer home in Whitehall, Michigan, a hamlet on White Lake on the west side of the state.

Claire had been a pretty, popular young woman. She met Bill Seldon one summer when she was going into her senior year of high school and Bill had just graduated from high school in Muskegon. He had a summer job at the White Lake Municipal Marina, and they had a summer romance that ended when Bill went off to the University of Michigan in Ann Arbor in the fall to study chemical engineering.

"Did you know him then?" Preuss asked.

"Not then," Roxanne Stewart said. "Claire told me about him, but I didn't meet him till later."

Claire had a variety of boys after her, Roxanne said, but she and Bill continued to write each other, and Claire visited him in Ann Arbor a few times during the school year. When she went to U of M after she graduated, she and Bill saw each other constantly.

Roxanne herself went away to Smith College, and while she and Claire were not in touch as often as they used to be, they still got together over school vacations.

"Claire seemed happy; she was in love. Or thought she was," Roxanne Stewart sniffed.

"You didn't care much for William Seldon?"

"I never trusted him. I always thought he was an opportunist."

He proposed when he was in his junior year of college, Roxanne continued, and he and Claire were married when he graduated. Claire, meanwhile, withdrew from school and concentrated on making a home for her new husband in Ferndale.

"I warned her not to do it," Roxanne said. "She'd always wanted to be a lawyer. But when she left school, she gave that up."

Her father's chemical company by that time had grown to the point where Curtis Johnson was able to take on Claire's new husband and slingshot him through the ranks from chemist to new product development manager to vice president of research and development before he was thirty.

By then, Claire had become pregnant and given birth to a son, Edward. The infant lived only a month.

"I don't think she ever recovered from the sadness of losing that child," Roxanne said. "Bill killed the baby, you know."

"I didn't."

"Well, as good as. Edward was born with spina bifida. He died after Bill told the doctors he wanted them to just 'let nature take its course,' without any medical intervention. Translation: Let the little cripple die."

Preuss had known too many parents of handicapped children who felt the same way—their children were no better than potted plants, embarrassing and humiliating defects of nature. He couldn't fathom that; he loved his son Toby so much, he couldn't imagine a life without him. He couldn't imagine Toby without a life.

"I read up on spina bifida," Roxanne continued, "and it could have been helped with surgery, even back then. The baby might have had some disabilities, but he would also have had a chance at a life. But that wasn't good enough for Bill Seldon. He had to be perfect. He had to be able to play football, take over the company when he was old enough, above all reflect glory back on Bill. Bill wouldn't accept a damaged child. He said that to Claire, point-blank. She never forgave him for it. I think that's when her dream of a happy family started to die."

Even so, Claire went on to have three other children, and dedicated herself to raising them and watching her husband's rapid climb through her father's company and the company's rapid international expansion.

"Until bad luck struck again," Roxanne said. "Claire developed a mastoid infection. When the surgeon operated, he found a growth on a nerve in her face. In the surgery to remove the growth, he nicked the nerve, which left one side of her face paralyzed. A specialist repaired the damage, but she still lost movement on the one side."

Preuss thought that explained her perpetually sour look in her photographs. Partial paralysis.

"She was terribly self-conscious about it," Roxanne said. "She was never a vain woman, but the botched surgery, even though it was mostly repaired, left her feeling homely. You couldn't even notice it unless you looked for it, but you couldn't convince her. She stopped going with Bill to his business functions, and she withdrew further and further into herself."

"When was the last time you saw her?" Preuss asked.

"We were in touch up to the day she was killed. But I think I was the only one she saw. By the end, she had pretty much cut herself off from everyone else who cared about her."

"Including her husband?"

She gave him a chilly smile. "I said everyone who cared about her."

"Which didn't include him, is that what you're saying?"

She shook her head. "I don't know if you know this, but Bill Seldon was an inveterate womanizer. He just couldn't keep it in his pants. And Claire knew all about it. She even told me a woman called Bill at their home one time."

"Claire spoke with a woman Seldon was seeing?"

"Yes. Is that brazen, or what? Neither one of them had any regard for Claire's feelings."

She turned her head at the sound of the front door opening. Heavy footsteps sounded in the living room and continued up the stairs to the second floor.

"That's my husband," she said. "He's going up to get changed. Mr. Preuss, if there isn't anything else, I have a gala to get to."

18

Back at his office, he closed his door to muffle the sound of Rhonda chatting with a man waiting to see Manny Greene. He had wanted to get a better sense of Claire Seldon, and now he had one . . . A terribly unhappy woman, suffering great physical and psychic pain, blatantly cheated on by her husband, and feeling a perpetual sense of loss over her first child.

A thought possessed him: Considering how unhappy she was, is it possible *she* was the one who arranged with Raymond Douglas to end her own life? Suicide by murder?

Even if she had been—which he had a hard time believing, though it was certainly possible, and it put a different spin on the facts of the case—the same problem existed for her as for her husband: How would she have gotten in touch with Ray Douglas?

He remembered he had left Jessie Douglas's yearbook in the Explorer. He went out to retrieve it and sat down to thumb through it.

It was a standard hard-cover high school yearbook, except there was a bar code and "Ferndale Public Library" stamp on the inside. Stolen from the library, probably.

He flipped to the page for Ray Douglas's homeroom, and found the group photo of the class. He looked for the stony face of Raymond Douglas. He looked at the other faces—children, as Dr. Portnoy had said, not even able to imagine what lay ahead for them in the years to come—and ran his finger along the italicized list of students' names below the photograph for Eugene Washburn.

Washburn looked like a smart-ass kid, with a mocking sneer and two close-set dark eyes staring off the page. He had the unfocused look of a stoner. Like the other boys in the photo, he wore a rumpled white shirt and badly knotted tie.

As he gazed into the wistful faces of the other students, he realized another face was circled in barely visible pencil.

Whoa.

He found the name that went with the face: A short stumpy kid in the second row, standing behind and to the right of Raymond Douglas. The kid had round shoulders and a round head with a mass of acne on his face and two prominent ears. Though he would soon have a growth spurt, he would never grow into those ears. He looked like he was about to cry.

Malcolm Seldon.

Was he also one of Raymond Douglas's cronies?

Dr. Portnoy didn't mention him. But even if not, they must have known each other. They were in the same homeroom, and in this photograph they were standing two feet apart. No one mentioned this connection before, certainly not Seldon himself.

In fact, Preuss remembered asking Malcolm Seldon directly about it, and Seldon said he'd never met Douglas. Yet here was proof they had to have been acquainted.

Interesting, that Malcolm Seldon went to school with the man who would go on to kill his mother. Ferndale's not that big a city, and there's only one high school. It stood to reason people in the same classroom and grade would know each other.

But why did Malcolm lie about it?

And was this what Jessie Douglas had told him she had recently found out? That her father went to school with a son of the woman her father killed? If so, what did that mean?

Preuss was too impatient to drive to Johnson Manufacturing and confront Seldon, so he called.

"Sorry," the receptionist said, "Mr. Seldon isn't available."

"Could you tell him it's urgent?" Preuss asked, annoyed.

"I spoke with his assistant, sir. He's at a meeting out of the building."

"Do you know when he'll be back?"

"Hang on."

She put him on hold, and ten seconds later was back on the phone. "He's expected later this afternoon."

"Do you have his cell number?"

"I'm sorry, I can't release that information."

He thought about that for a moment. "What about Lawrence Seldon?"

"He's also out of the building."

He thanked her and disconnected. He sat for a moment, then closed up his office.

"I'm off," he told Rhonda Citron.

"Where to?"

"See a man about a car."

Washburn Buick was a concrete and smoked glass rectangle sur-rounded by car lots half a mile up Woodward from 8 Mile Road in Ferndale. Inside the showroom, a salesman approached him and Preuss asked to see Eugene Washburn. The salesman eyed him up and down and told him to wait a moment and he'd see if the boss was free.

Preuss wandered around the gleaming new cars, fending off four different salespeople, until a man in a polo shirt and khaki trousers walked out from the back warren of offices, followed by the salesman whom Preuss first talked to. The salesman pointed out Preuss, and the man in the polo shirt walked over with his hand out-stretched.

"Gene Washburn," he said. Preuss recognized the two beady eyes from his high school photo but the dark shock of hair had reced-ed dramatically.

They shook hands and Preuss introduced himself. "Is there someplace we can talk?"

"Sure," Washburn said. "What's this about?"

Preuss handed him his business card and said, "Raymond Douglas."

Washburn at first gave him a blank look, then understanding spread across his face. He said, "Follow me," and led Preuss back through a warren of offices to a glassed-in conference room with a whiteboard covered in scrawled monthly sales figures, and a cutout figure of a cartoon salesman on whose belly was listed names beside numbers of vehicle units sold.

Washburn indicated a chair at the oval conference table and Preuss sat. Washburn closed the door and said, "Get you some coffee?"

"I'm good, thanks."

Washburn sat adjacent to Preuss and laid his phone on the table in front of him. Immediately the phone vibrated with a text. Washburn picked up the phone, checked the screen, and set it back down.

"My salesman thought you were from the police," he said.

"I'm a retired Ferndale PD detective."

"Must still carry the look about you," Washburn said with an oily grin. "Anyway, I thought I'd seen you before. Community events and so forth."

When Preuss didn't reply, Washburn said, "So Raymond Douglas. Man, I haven't heard that name in years."

"You knew he went to prison for murder?"

"I remember that trial. I knew Ray in high school. I wasn't surprised he came to a bad end. I guess I was shocked I actually knew somebody who committed murder."

"I heard you and Ray ran together in high school."

Washburn tilted his head back, gave a mirthless smile. "Who told you that?"

Preuss ignored the question. "You knew him, though, correct?"

"Well, sure," Washburn said. "We all knew about Raymond."

"What did you know?"

"He was a bad apple."

"Did you have much to do with him?"

"Like I say, everybody knew he was trouble. Most of us tried to keep away from him."

"Gene," Preuss said, leaning forward and lowering his voice as though speaking confidentially, deploying the police trick of using

Washburn's familiar first name, "let me tell you what I know. I know you were the ringleader—and that's the word that was used, ringleader—of a group of troublemakers in high school. And one of those was Ray Douglas."

Washburn looked at Preuss as though he had pulled out a large handgun and pointed it at Washburn's head.

Washburn's phone vibrated with another text. He let it buzz on the table without attending to it.

"I also know you all had juvenile records, which were sealed. So let's set aside the innocent lamb routine so I can get some answers, okay, Gene?"

Washburn looked at him without saying anything. Swallowed hard.

"I'm not here to rake up any old troubles," Preuss continued. "Or cause any new ones. I'm looking into the crime Ray Douglas was convicted of, and I'm trying to see if you can help me."

"I thought that was all settled years ago."

"There are still some questions."

"Even after all this time?"

Preuss nodded.

Washburn sighed. "Can I just tell you, though, I'm not that kid anymore."

"Everybody grows up."

Washburn acknowledged the truth of that with a nod. "I sowed a lot of wild oats back then. All through college, too, if you want to know the truth. But I straightened myself out. All behind me. No need to look in the rear-view."

If you're a ne'er-do-well, it helps if Daddy has a business you can step into, Preuss thought. Like a car dealership. Or a chemical company.

"When was the last time you saw Ray Douglas?"

"Not since high school. Must be at least twenty years."

"You haven't spoken with him since then?"

Washburn's phone vibrated twice with two more texts. He checked his screen, then laid the phone back down. Preuss glared at him, and he moved the phone away.

"No," he said. "I saw him on TV when he was caught and went on trial. But I haven't talked with him since he left school. After that, he kind of faded from everybody's sight. I heard he went into the army, and when he came out, all that terrible stuff happened. But that's all I know about him."

"Sounds like he was pretty messed up in high school."

"We all were. Maybe Ray more than the others, because most of the rest of us, we all came from money, and Ray's family was dirt poor. That made a difference."

"So, what, that made him even more messed up?"

"No," Washburn said, "but he seemed to have a different attitude about everything. My parents were totally unhinged when the cops picked me up. Which happened more times than I care to admit. But he only had his mother, as I recall, and for her it was like, eh, no biggie."

Preuss thought about what Dr. Portnoy had said—Ray's mother was always drunk, never engaged in her son's life.

"What were you picked up for?"

"Petty stuff, compared to what's going on with kids today. With us it was vandalism, shoplifting from Hudson's, shit like that. But Ray, he went further. Stole a car, if I'm not mistaken. We thought he was a big-time criminal."

"So you haven't seen him since your high school days?"

"No."

"And you lost track of him after he left school, except for seeing him on television?"

"Correct."

"And you have no knowledge of how he got involved with the kidnapping and murder?"

"No idea."

"There's a rumor going around, somebody may have helped Ray with the kidnapping."

Washburn shrugged and said, "News to me."

"You never heard anything about that? Maybe from the other members of your little gang?"

"Never.

"Did you know anyone else he ran with?"

"If I ever did, I've forgotten by now."

"What about Malcolm Seldon?"

"What about him?"

"You knew him in high school, too, right?"

"We had some classes together."

"Was he part of your crowd?"

"Malcolm? No way."

"Why do you say it that way?"

"Let's just say Malcolm was always a goody two-shoes. Straight-A student, student government type."

"And you were the rebels?"

"In our own fashion, yeah."

"Have you been in touch with Malcolm since high school?"

"Sure. We see each other around."

"Where?"

"Different events around town. We're businessmen in the same city, so we travel in some of the same circles."

"Yes, but have you spoken?"

"Sure," Washburn said. "We say hello and chat about this and that. Local business conditions and so forth."

"Ever talk about his mother's death?"

"Certainly not. I never mention it, and he never brings it up. We're not that close. Besides, it's all old news."

"Not any more," Preuss said. He stood. "Thanks for your time."

"Sorry I couldn't be more help."

Washburn put his phone in his pocket and opened the conference room door for Preuss. A woman was waiting to rush up with a fistful of phone messages. "Urgent," she said.

Washburn took the messages and shoved them in his khaki pocket. "Come on," he told Preuss, "I'll walk you out."

He led Preuss back through the offices, past customers sitting in tiny cubicles having deep discussions with salesmen.

At the front entrance, Preuss and Washburn shook hands.

"By the way," Preuss said, "if you didn't run with Malcolm Seldon, who else was in your little gang?"

Washburn smiled as he thought back to the old crowd. "There was me, and Ray, and Joe Venarian, Sandra Winters, and Carolyn Kwiatkowske. We were troublemakers." He laughed softly, remembering his carefree days. "We weren't a gang, exactly. We were all too middle-class for that. Well, except Ray, like I said. But we caused our share of havoc."

"They still in the area?"

"Joe works for GM. Last I heard from him—which was last Christmas—he was working overseas at guh-moo."

"What's 'guh-moo'?"

"That's what he called GM Overseas Operations. He's some big honcho for them."

"What about Sandra Winters and Carolyn Kwiatkowske?"

"I married Sandra. And Carolyn I see all the time."

"She lives in the area?"

"Sure. You've probably seen her, too."

"How so?"

"Ever watch the local news?"

"Not if I can help it."

"Tune into Channel 4 news sometime. Six and eleven, you'll see her. She uses a different name, though. Kwiatkowske has a nice ethnic flavor, but she thought it would be too hard to pronounce, especially for some of the idiots who anchor the news. Now she calls herself Carrie Kaye."

19

He tried Carrie Kaye from the Explorer in the dealership parking lot. Her phone message said she was either in the field or on the air, and invited him to leave a message or punch "five" if the call was urgent and required immediate attention. He punched in the number and was transferred to the message system for the news department's administrative assistant, who wasn't in either.

So much for immediate attention.

He left a message, then called Carrie Kaye's direct number again and asked her to call him as soon as she got the message.

He sat in the Explorer for a few minutes, trying to put all the new pieces together—who knew whom, who denied knowing whom, who *was* whom . . .

His phone rang. Carrie Kaye's administrative assistant, calling back.

Preuss left the Explorer in the parking structure next to the Millender Center apartments downtown on Brush Street and walked across the skyway to the Coleman Young Municipal Building at the foot of Woodward, near the Detroit River. He took the elevator to the thirteenth floor, where the City Council held their meetings. In the hallway outside the main chambers, a battery of television news reporters along with radio and print journalists were doing stand-ups with various Council members.

Carrie Kaye's assistant said the reporter would be here, covering the City Council president's latest public relations fiasco. The president was found to be spending city funds on his personal health regimen instead of on Detroit's deepening financial crisis.

The voices echoed off the marble walls and floor. Preuss saw a news team with a Channel 4 logo on the ENG camera and headed toward them. A woman stood in a pool of light, talking with one of the Council members, a man known for making flamboyantly stupid remarks on any subject he was asked about. She held a microphone in front of the Councilman's face and the bright white of the camera's light made him squint. Preuss wouldn't recognize Carrie Kaye, but he assumed this was her.

He waited as she wrapped up the interview and turned to face the camera for her final words. Preuss couldn't hear what she was saying, but her pretentious sonority carried down the hall. She had long glossy brown hair that hung down over one shoulder and a thin face with a bony jaw.

She finished her wind-up, said, "Carrie Kaye, Channel 4 News. Ted?" She waited a few beats, and then said, "Cut it," and the cameraman turned off his ENG rig and shut down the light.

Preuss made his way between the other reporters. "Carrie Kaye?"

She turned to face him. "Yes?" Her look was stern, prepared to fend off whatever he wanted.

He handed her a business card. "Martin Preuss. We spoke the other day about Jessie Douglas."

She examined the card. "Okay."

"She was trying to gin up interest in her father's story. He'd just died in prison and—"

"I remember you," she interrupted. "You asked about her. But I told you I couldn't help."

"Now I need to ask you about somebody else."

She raised her eyebrows in polite disinterest.

"Malcolm Seldon," Preuss said.

He let that sink in for a few seconds. He could see sudden activity behind her eyes.

"Why do you want to know about him?"

Preuss said, "Is there someplace we can talk?"

She handed her microphone to her cameraman. "Nick, give me a few minutes, okay?"

Nick nodded, but pointed to his watch. "Still gotta edit this," he reminded her.

"Wait here, okay? Five minutes."

She opened the nearest door and led Preuss into a cavernous empty auditorium that sloped upward from the front of the room. She sat in one of the spectator chairs, and he took one two seats away.

"How well do you know Malcolm?"

She raised a nonchalant shoulder. "We've met."

"You've known each other since high school, isn't that right?"

"*High* school? Okay, I've known him since high school. What does that have to do with anything? I haven't seen him recently."

"Really." More statement than question.

"Really," she said.

"I've just come from speaking with Eugene Washburn."

"So? I knew Eugene, too. High school was a long time ago."

"Carrie," he said, "you seem a little nervous here."

She glanced at her watch. "Look, I have a deadline to make."

"When was the last time you saw Malcolm? And don't say high school, because I don't believe you."

"Why are you so interested in this?"

"Please answer the question."

"I don't see what this has to do with anything. And it's certainly none of your business."

"Listen," Preuss said, "in your line of work, I'm sure you've heard every possible way to avoid answering a straight question. But none of them are going to work with me. Please tell me when you last saw Malcolm Seldon."

"Or what? I resent being spoken to like this."

"Resent all you want. The longer you take to answer, the more I'll think you have something to hide."

An electric jolt seemed to shoot through her spine. She bit back the next thing she was going to say. "Okay," she said finally, "I did speak with Malcolm recently."

"When?"

"I don't appreciate your tone."

Whatever made her sit up also turned the light on for him. "I don't care what's going on between you, Carrie."

She didn't know how to respond to that. Finally, she said, "I thought that's what all this was about."

"It's not. All I'm interested in is what you told him about Jessie Douglas."

It took her a few seconds to realign her comprehension. She gave her hair a flip. "How do you know I told him anything?"

"Please," he said. "What did you tell him?"

"I thought he deserved to know she was asking questions about his family."

"When was this?"

"Last week."

"How'd he take the news?"

"He was upset."

"Did he seem frightened of anything?"

"No. More angry."

"Did he say what he was going to do with the information?"

"No."

"That's all you told him? Jessie Douglas was asking questions?"

"He asked me for details."

"And what did you tell him?"

"Just what she told me. Her father said somebody put him up to the job he went away for. She wanted to find out who."

"Why didn't you tell me about this when I asked you?"

"Look," she said, "I didn't know you, and it was about people I care for."

He considered that, and nodded, even though he didn't believe her.

"We were seeing each other," she said, though he didn't ask. "Malcolm and I, I mean. But it's been over for a while."

He held up a hand to stop her. "Not interested."

"So can I go now?"

Instead of answering, Preuss said, "You know she's dead, right?"

"Who?"

"Jessie Douglas."

"She's *dead*?" She grimaced in horror. "How——?"

"Somebody killed her."

Carrie stared at him.

"Don't tell me you haven't heard that," Preuss said. "Malcolm didn't tell you?"

"No. I had no idea."

For somebody in the news business, you're a little behind the times, he thought.

"When was this?" she asked.

"Sunday night."

She tried to process that. "Do they know who did it?"

"Not yet," Preuss said. "They'll find out."

"You don't think Malcolm——?"

He shrugged. He let her think about that for another few beats.

Nick the cameraman stuck his head inside the auditorium and said, "Carrie? Gotta go."

She threw Preuss a last searching look. Then she gave her hair a final flip and left him alone in the auditorium.

20

"I found a connection in Jessie Douglas's murder," Preuss told Reg Trombley from the Explorer. "Might be important." He sped north on the I-75 expressway toward Ferndale from downtown Detroit.

"Malcolm Seldon went to school with Ray Douglas," Preuss continued, "and Malcolm knew Jessie Douglas was asking questions about who helped her father."

"How'd you find that out?"

"One of their classmates in high school is a reporter for Channel 4. Carrie Kaye. Jessie asked her to do a story on her father, and the reporter told Malcolm."

"Then right after that, Jessie turns up dead."

"Yeah."

As Preuss knew he would, Trombley caught the implications immediately. It put Malcolm front and center for Jessie's death and as Ray Douglas's mystery accomplice—the first to cover up the second.

"Not looking good for Malcolm, all of a sudden," Trombley said.

"No."

"Where are you now?"

"On my way to Johnson Manufacturing to talk to him. I'm twenty minutes away."

"Meet you there," Trombley said.

The guest parking lot at the Johnson facility was full, and the security guard in the kiosk around the back wouldn't let him park in the employee lot. So Preuss left the Explorer illegally parked on West End behind Trombley's Taurus and trotted up to the front door.

The receptionist buzzed him in. Trombley was leaning over the counter, speaking with her.

"What's happening?" Preuss asked.

"Ms. Kachadorian here says Malcolm is gone for the day."

"Already? It's only—" Preuss looked at his watch. 4:30. He was shocked to discover it was so late. "When did he leave?"

"We just missed him. He busted out about a half hour ago."

Right after Carrie Kaye called him to let him know we talked, Preuss figured.

"He say where he was going?"

Ms. Kachadorian shook her head regretfully. "Sorry."

"Do you have his home address?"

"I'm not allowed to give that out."

"Never mind," Trombley said. "I'll find it in two minutes."

Preuss thanked the young woman and followed Trombley, who walked away from the reception counter as he punched in a number on his cell. He listened for a moment, then shook his head. "Records' number is busy." He punched in another number.

"Hank," Trombley said into the phone, casting a glance at Preuss, "got a minute for a favor?"

Trombley listened, made the "yak-yak-yak" sign with his fingers and thumb, then said, "Yeah, Hank, I'm sure you're jammed. All I want is, check the DMV records for an address. Take you a minute." He spelled out Malcolm Seldon's name, and waited.

He threw Preuss an ironic wink. Hank Bellamy, another detective in the Bureau, had done everything he could to undermine Preuss when they worked together before Preuss retired. If Bellamy knew this would help Preuss, he never would have found the time for it.

Preuss heard Bellamy's voice come back on the line, and Trombley said, "Great, thanks. Text it to me?"

He disconnected and they waited. "Hank says hi," Trombley said.

"Give him my best."

In another few seconds, Trombley's phone chimed. "That's it. Address in Bingham Farms." Trombley texted the information to Preuss's phone.

"Let's go," Preuss said.

"You go on. I have to liaise with the local force. You remember how that goes."

"Do what you have to. I'm off."

Working private has its benefits after all, Preuss thought as he trotted back to the Explorer, unencumbered by territoriality.

Malcolm Seldon lived in a contemporary tri-level in a wooded area in the prosperous northwest suburb.

A frantic woman pulled the door open as Preuss approached the front steps. "Thank God you're here," she cried. "Come in, please!"

She pulled him inside and said, "My husband's upstairs, in his study. Please hurry!"

She ran up the curving stairway with Preuss on her heels.

"What's going on?" he asked.

"Didn't they tell you?"

"Who?"

"Your dispatcher. Or whoever sends you out."

"I'm not a police officer, ma'am."

"You're not?"

She stopped at the top of the stairs. "Who are you? I called 911, they said they'd be right here. I thought you were them."

"I'm a private investigator. I came over to talk with your husband."

"Come on, then. He's in here. Please *hurry*!"

They stopped in front of a closed door. She tried the handle. Locked.

She tapped on the door. "Malcolm? Honey, please open the door. There's somebody here to see you."

No sound from inside the room.

"What's happening?" Preuss asked.

"He got home from work a little while ago. He looked terrible. He yelled at me and then came up here and locked himself in his study."

"Do you have a spare key to the room?"

"No. I thought I did." She produced a small key from her Levis pocket. "He must have changed the lock. This doesn't work."

"Maybe he just needs some time to cool down. What's the problem?"

"The problem is," she said, as though Preuss were thick, "he has a *gun* in there. And he's threatening to use it on himself. Look, can you do something about this? He needs *help!*"

Preuss knocked on the door. "Malcolm? It's Martin Preuss. Can you let me in so we can talk about this?"

No response, until Seldon's eerily calm voice said, "Go away."

"Your wife's pretty upset. How about you unlock the door and we'll talk about it."

When there was no response, Preuss knocked again. "Open the door, Malcolm. Can you open up? Let's talk."

After a moment, Preuss heard movement, then the click of a lock. The door swung open a few inches.

Preuss nudged it the rest of the way with his foot.

A conventional home office, a man cave for an office worker with a large desk facing the wall and a long sofa and coffee table, as if Seldon had duplicated his work space here. Seldon was backing up and reaching behind him to find the sofa. He held a pistol in his hand.

Pointed under his own chin.

"Shut the door," he said.

Preuss closed the door and turned with his hands up, as if Seldon were aiming at him instead of himself.

"Malcolm," Preuss said, "you don't want to do this."

"Oh, I do," Seldon said in the same eerie even tone. "I most certainly do." He sat back on the sofa, still with the gun aimed under his chin.

Preuss edged closer and Seldon pointed the gun out at him. "Don't."

"Okay. Okay." Preuss stopped, backed off a foot.

Seldon pointed the gun barrel back at his head.

"Why are you doing this?"

"Don't you know?"

"No," Preuss said. "Can you tell me?"

Preuss heard sirens as police cruisers pulled into the driveway outside, then cut off. Malcolm turned his head toward the window, and Preuss saw a mix of emotions flit over his face: Disappointment, relief, and, briefly, hopefulness.

Then fury.

"You better keep them away from me," Malcolm shouted.

"They just want to help—"

"I said keep them away!"

"Okay, okay. Your wife's right here. I'll let her know."

His hands still up, Preuss backed toward the door to the hall. "Mrs. Seldon?"

"Here," she said. Preuss opened the door, and she started into the room. Malcolm shouted, "Keep out!" when he saw her.

Preuss urged her back. "Malcolm," she cried, "why are you doing this?"

The doorbell rang downstairs, then a pounding on the front door. Everything happening at once.

"Listen—listen," Preuss said, trying to pierce through the frantic woman's attention. "Go downstairs and tell the police not to come up yet. Okay? Do you understand? Give me a little more time with him."

"Why is he doing this?"

More pounding on the front door.

"I don't know. Go downstairs. Don't let them come up. Okay? He doesn't want them up here."

She nodded, and rushed down the stairs.

Preuss edged back into Seldon's room. "Okay, Malcolm. They're not coming. Your wife went to talk with them."

"Shut the door."

Preuss closed the door and eased toward Seldon again.

"Stay there."

Preuss stopped. "Not going to do anything. I just want to talk."

Seldon closed his eyes, swallowed hard, the gun still under his chin. He seemed to be trying to gin up the courage to pull the trigger.

"Can I sit down?" Preuss asked.

"No! Stay where you are."

"Okay. Okay. Malcolm, is this because Carrie called you?"

Seldon nodded. "She said you asked about me. And you told her the Douglas woman was dead."

"But you already knew that, didn't you?"

"Yes," Seldon admitted.

Preuss was certain he didn't tell Malcolm when they first spoke on the morning her body was found. How else would he know, unless he killed her?

"Carrie told you Jessie was around," Preuss said. "Asking questions about her father."

"Yes."

"You knew him, didn't you? Ray Douglas."

Seldon raised his head and gave Preuss a doleful nod.

Slowly, Preuss squatted on his heels, still with his hands up.

"But what's all this"—he spread his hands, taking in the scene that Seldon had created in his office—"have to do with that, Malcolm? Can you tell me?"

Seldon didn't look at Preuss, but Preuss could tell he had the other man's attention.

"Can you help me understand? What's the connection? Why are you doing this?"

Seldon looked at Preuss. He let his gun hand drift away from his head, but Preuss didn't dare move.

"I didn't mean for it to happen," Seldon said. "I swear."

"I know, Malcolm." Thinking Seldon was talking about killing Jessie Douglas. "Tell me what happened. Was it an accident?"

Seldon shook his head. "No accident." But Preuss couldn't tell if he was responding to Preuss's question or to another voice in his head, one only he could hear.

"I didn't know he was going to do it," Seldon murmured.

"Who was going to do what? You didn't know Ray was going to kill your mother?"

Seldon shook his head, waving that idea away wildly with his gun hand. "No. No!" He let the gun rest on his knee.

"Who are you talking about?"

"I didn't know he was going to *kill* that girl."

"Jessie? You didn't know who was going to kill her? *Who* was going to kill Jessie?"

"You don't know?"

"No."

"It was me," Seldon said. "I killed her. And I don't think I can live with it."

There we are, Preuss thought. The stress must be causing him to disassociate and refer to himself in the third person.

He watched as Seldon's face melted into tears with an explosive sob.

Yet seeing him, Preuss felt something about this wasn't right. Trombley told him Malcolm had an alibi for the night Jessie was killed. Even if that didn't hold up, could Malcolm summon the anger or insanity necessary to kill Jessie Douglas? Anybody could do anything under the right circumstances, but suddenly Preuss doubted it.

"Malcolm, I don't think you did."

Seldon wiped his eyes with his sleeve. "I may as well have."

"But somebody else killed her, not you. Right?"

Seldon nodded.

"I told him what that girl was doing," Seldon said. "Showing up asking about her father. As soon as Carrie told me, I told him."

He pounded his gun hand on his knee. "I *told* him, don't you get it?"

In a flash, Preuss did.

"Lolly," he said.

The family nickname for Malcolm and Mary's older brother.

"You told your brother Jessie Douglas was here. And then he killed her?"

Seldon nodded. He was too overwhelmed to speak.

"When did you tell him?"

Seldon took a breath, regained control. "Dad's birthday party."

The Sunday night Jessie was killed. Right after she talked to Preuss about handling her case.

But why? Why would Lawrence Seldon kill the daughter of the man who killed their mother? For revenge? Out of spite?

"But look," Preuss said, "this isn't your fault. You didn't kill her, Malcolm. Whatever your brother did, it's not your fault."

"It *is*," Seldon insisted. "I told him about her. He wanted me to set up a meeting with her. So I did. On the night of Dad's party."

So Lawrence Seldon must have slipped away from the party. A fact everyone failed to mention.

"But he told me they were just going to talk," Seldon went on. "So he could persuade her there wasn't any truth in what her father told her."

"So Lolly met her. And that's when he killed her?"

Seldon nodded. "He told me he was just going to talk to her," he murmured. "Convince her to stop asking her questions. But she wouldn't. She wasn't going to stop."

"You're not to blame for what happened after that, Malcolm."

"I *am!*" Malcolm cried. "What's the matter with you? Don't you see, she'd still be alive if I'd just kept quiet."

A look of determination twisted Seldon's face. It charged the air in the room, dropped the temperature twenty degrees. The hairs rose on the back of Preuss's neck and he felt rather than knew what was going to happen.

As though in slow motion, Seldon raised the gun to his chin and as he did Preuss launched himself across the six feet separating them. Arms outstretched, Preuss dove at the gun in Seldon's right hand.

Not in time. The boom of the shot exploded in Preuss's ear.

Momentarily deafened, he didn't hear the thunder of the Bingham Farms police rushing up the stairs, or the commotion in the room once they saw what happened. He heard only the echoing cottony hum in his ears, and saw only the blood spattered over his hands and arms and shirt.

And the side of Malcolm Seldon's face.

21

But Seldon wasn't dead.

With his desperate lunge, Preuss jostled Seldon's gun enough for the bullet to crease but not penetrate his skull. The Bingham Farms cops called for an emergency vehicle, and the EMTs hustled Seldon out of the house and off to Beaumont Hospital's Royal Oak location. He was still breathing but unconscious.

Outside, Trombley stood beside his friend and former colleague as Preuss gave a statement to a Bingham Farms detective. The detective knew Preuss from his days on the Ferndale force and showed him some deference, as though he were still part of the tribe.

Afterward, Trombley sat with Preuss in the Explorer while Preuss—ears still ringing—related what Seldon had told him.

"He told you flat-out his brother killed Jessie Douglas?" Trombley asked.

"Yes."

"You believe him?"

"I do. He tried to kill himself because he thought he was to blame for it."

"Did he say why?"

"He said he told his brother about Jessie, then his brother went to meet her and he killed her. That's when Malcolm tried to shoot himself in the head."

"Nice work stopping that, by the way."

Preuss accepted it with a shake of his own head. "It felt like it took an hour to get across the room to him."

"So," Trombley said, "Lawrence killed Jessie Douglas because Malcolm told him Jessie was asking questions. Which he obviously didn't want to happen."

"For a second in there," Preuss said, "I thought Lawrence killed her because he was trying to avenge his mother's death somehow. Or to punish Jessie."

"For the sins of her father."

"But that doesn't make sense," Preuss said. "Ray Douglas was dead—Jessie's death couldn't hurt him. And Jessie was a child when Claire Seldon died. Why punish her for that?"

"What's your gut tell you?"

"Larry was the one who abetted his father in his mother's murder. And he didn't want that found out."

"That's assuming the father actually was involved in the death of his first wife," Trombley pointed out.

"I think he was," Preuss said. "I think he wanted to be free from his first wife to marry the woman he was seeing. So he arranged for somebody to kill her. And Larry helped him. Then to protect his father, Larry killed Jessie Douglas."

"That's cold."

"But what I haven't worked out yet is why. Why go to the trouble of killing his wife?"

"To save himself a massive divorce settlement? Lots of money in that family."

"Maybe," Preuss said.

"You don't sound convinced."

"No. That's nuts."

"What Malcolm told you should be enough for a warrant for his brother," Trombley said. "Maybe he can give us some answers. I'll get it going with the ADA."

Preuss went back to his office. Rhonda and Manny were both gone. The office was silent and dark—just the peace he needed after this day.

On his desk was the high school yearbook for Ray Douglas and the rest of the actors in this drama. Whatever had happened between Ray Douglas, Malcolm Seldon, and Carrie Kaye had its start here, he thought as he held the slender book in his hands.

He thumbed through it, looking again for the homeroom page for Douglas and the others. High school was not a particularly happy time for Preuss, either at school or at home, where his alcoholic father clashed regularly with his drug-addled older brother. Preuss had just wanted it to be over as fast as possible. He never took part in sports, or any of the other activities whose photos filled yearbooks like this one. When each day at school was finished, he would head home and play his guitar, shut up in his room. It was the only thing that kept him close to sane. The only thing he could control.

He found the page with the homeroom photograph. Carolyn Kwiatkowske wasn't in their room, but he looked again at Ray Douglas, Malcolm Seldon, Eugene Washburn, and, standing next to Washburn, a slender, long-nosed young woman whom the caption identified as Sandra Winters. The future Mrs. Washburn.

He rifled through the rest of the book. There were the usual photos of the most popular students, and shots of athletic teams, the French Club, the Spanish Club, the Future Teachers Club, the Drama Club, and so on. And the usual sentimental quotes from the graduating seniors about how their high school days would be the most important of their lives, and they would remember their friends forever.

Yeah, right. Preuss was in touch with exactly nobody from high school.

To his surprise, he also saw several photos of Raymond Douglas in the yearbook, more than he would have guessed would be there for an alienated kid like Ray. And in many, Douglas was with the same young woman—dark hair feathered in the Farrah Fawcett style of the times, a heavy, curvaceous young woman, happy and smiling. There they were at the Homecoming dance, doing what passed for dancing to what passed for music in the mid-1980s; there they were at a football game in the field behind the high school, mugging for the photographer with their arms around each other; there they were in a classroom, sitting side-by-side, sharing the same math book.

There they were in a series of candid shots in the school corridors, having an intense tete-a-tete, laughing together at something someone—a young Eugene Washburn, Preuss realized—had just said in the cafeteria, all captured for eternity in the flash of the camera. There they were posing together beside a pine tree in the snow out on the school grounds, dreamy young lovers imagining a life together that would never happen.

In these moments, Preuss thought Ray Douglas looked happy, so different from the image Preuss had formed of an angry, tormented, rebellious young man.

Who was the girl who made him feel that way?

The photo of them at the Homecoming dance had a caption. He read it and slammed the desk with his fist.

The pieces of the case realigned, tiles on a floor reordering themselves in a pattern different from the one he had suspected.

22

He heard the dog's high-pitched yapping as he stood in the building's hallway. Preuss felt a presence gather behind the door. He could almost hear the woman's thoughts as she peered through the peep hole.

Mary Seldon swung the door open, took a look at his face, nodded once, as though confirming to herself why he was there, and stepped aside so he could enter. She led the way into the galley kitchen of her condo. "Coffee?" she asked.

"Sure."

"Have a seat."

He sat on a high-backed chair at the dining room table beside the kitchen. He watched her pour fresh water into her coffee maker and set a new coffee pod in the machine.

When a cup was full and steaming, she set it in front of him. "You take it black, right?"

"Right."

She nodded and prepared her own coffee.

When that was ready, she sat across the table from him. She took a sip, sighed, and waited for him to begin.

He placed Jessie Douglas's pilfered copy of the Ferndale High School yearbook on the table between them. He opened to a page he had marked with a Post-it. It was the page with the photo of Ray and his date at the Homecoming dance.

He tapped the picture. "Ray Douglas," Preuss said. "And that's you."

The caption read:

At the Homecoming party, lovebirds Mary Seldon and Ray Douglas celebrate the team's gridiron triumph with a victory dance.

She studied it, then looked away. She pursed her lips and began the process of lighting a cigarette with trembling hands.

"You and Ray were a couple," Preuss said. "'Lovebirds,' right?"

She acknowledged that with a sigh and took a deep draw on her smoke. She seemed to be searching for something to say, some way to respond to this eruption from her past.

Preuss thought again of a quote from his college days: The past is never dead, William Faulkner wrote; it's not even past.

Now Mary took another look at the photo, gave a mirthless smile. "See how heavy I was? I took all that weight off after graduation. But Ray liked me the way I was back then, so . . ." Her voice trailed off.

"Why didn't you tell me?"

"About Ray and me?"

"Yes."

She took a few moments before answering. "It seems so long ago," she said. "So much water under the bridge." She reached out and ran a fingertip along Ray's photo, as though caressing his face with the unpolished tip of her slender finger.

"How long did it last?"

"Just till he left school. Then we drifted apart. You know how these things go," she said. "They're the most important things in your life, until they're not. We saw each other a few times after he dropped out, but he'd already moved on to another kind of life."

The life that would bring him Jessie Douglas, Preuss thought.

"Mary," Preuss said, "what wasn't clear to me from the trial transcripts was why he picked your mother. He claimed it was random, but he told his daughter somebody directed him toward your mother. Isn't there anything you can tell me about that?"

She shook her head and stared at her coffee cup.

He kept looking at her, but she avoided his gaze.

"Did someone from your family reach out to Ray?" he asked quietly. "Is that how he got mixed up in this?"

She tapped the ash off her cigarette. She kept tapping even though all that was left was the glowing end.

She nodded.

"Who was it?"

She looked up at him, and he knew the answer.

"It was you," he said.

She nodded again.

"Did your father ask you to do it?" he asked. "Because he knew Ray was somebody who could do what he wanted done with your mother?"

"No. My father never asked me to do that."

"Then who did?"

She was silent for a full minute.

Then, without looking at him, she said, "Lolly."

"Did you know why?"

"No. I didn't know what they had in mind, or whose idea it was. Honestly, I don't think Lolly did either, at the time."

She looked at him with tragic eyes.

"It's hard to believe now, I know. But back then, the only thing Lolly told me was, the company needed somebody to do some special job. He asked if I could put him in touch with Ray. He said he didn't want to do it himself because Ray thought Lolly hated him. And it was true, the whole family hated Ray. They thought he was trash."

"But you did put Ray in touch with your brother?"

"Yes," she said. "I told Ray my brother wanted to talk with him about a job. Ray was in a terrible state when he came home from the army. As crazy as he was, I thought this would help settle him. And it gave me an excuse to see him again, which I wanted to do. I suppose some part of me hoped we could rekindle what we'd had before."

She sighed at the futility of her own behavior. "I was young. And stupid. But by then I didn't know him anymore. He was a different person."

"In what way?"

She fingered the handle of her coffee cup. "Angrier. Crazier. I don't know if it was PTSD from the war, or just all his emotional problems worsening in his old environment, but he was nuts. Ranting about the government, seeing enemies behind every lamppost. You heard the story he told about why he kidnapped my mother?"

"He wanted to be the chief of police of Ferndale?"

"He disavowed that at the trial. He said it was the first thing that came to mind when he was picked up. But it was true. He even told me he wanted to be police chief when I saw him that time about getting in touch with Lolly."

She looked at Preuss and he could see she was was fighting a losing battle with tears. "So I was the one who put Ray Douglas on the path to killing my mother."

"And all this time, you've blamed yourself for causing your mother's death."

"Since the day they arrested Ray for her murder, I've barely thought about anything else."

Preuss considered the burden of guilt she had been living with for all these years. No wonder her mother's death hit her so hard.

And no wonder her life went to hell and never really came back.

And no wonder brother Lolly didn't want Preuss to speak with her. Because of what her guilt might compel her to reveal.

"But you didn't know at the time who asked your brother to contact Ray? Or if it was his own idea?"

"I always assumed it was my father. Both brothers would have done anything my father told them to. I asked my father about it once. I specifically asked him if he was the one who got Lolly to ask Ray to kill my mother."

"And?"

She took a sip of coffee, as though fortifying herself against the answer.

"This was a few years after my mother died. By then, his cognitive problems were even worse than they had been before she died. I'm not sure he even understood what I was asking him."

"Your father was having cognitive problems all the way back then?"

She nodded. "That's why he retired from the company. The official story was that he left to make way for the next generation. But the truth was, he just couldn't handle it any more. His Alzheimer's made it too hard to function. He was forgetful, he couldn't make decisions, he couldn't process information, he couldn't recognize his staff from one day to the next. He barely knew his own family, some days. That was why my mother was going to reorganize the company before she died, and take it public."

"Sorry—what did you just say?"

"Before she was killed, she had a plan to reorganize the company and take it public."

This was the first he had heard of that. "Say more about that, would you?"

"The company was privately held, and when Grandpa Johnson died, he deliberately left it solely to her. By then, he'd had enough of my father's womanizing."

"I've heard about that," Preuss said.

"So my mother wanted to get my father out of the picture, in part because of his cognitive problems, which were getting worse, but also because of his behavior with other women. She didn't even want the business to go to my brothers, because she knew they'd still do whatever he wanted them to. And I was too young, and too uninterested. If she took it public, with a new board of directors and a new CEO, she could make sure my father would be out."

"Apparently that didn't happen."

"No," Mary said. "She died before she could make it happen. So he got the company after all."

"Who else knew about this?"

"No one, to my knowledge. I was the only one in the family she trusted."

"And you didn't mention it to anyone?"

She shook her head.

"The word must have leaked out somehow," Preuss said. "That kind of thing is hard to keep secret."

She shrugged.

That could be William Seldon's motive for getting rid of his wife, Preuss thought. That could be the missing piece.

"Did this come out at the trial?" he asked. He didn't remember seeing anything about it in the transcripts. "Nobody suspected your father might be involved?"

"They caught Ray right away," she said. "I'm not sure why he didn't mention anything."

Because he was struggling with his own demons, Preuss thought.

"So," Preuss said, thinking out loud, "when Jessie Douglas talked about someone putting her father up to the kidnapping, you believed it was your father."

"I believed he arranged this, yes. Mr. Preuss," she continued, "I've spent my whole adult life regretting what I did for my family. Or for my father and brothers, I should say. My mother paid dearly for my weakness. As far as I'm concerned, the only co-conspirator you need to be concerned about is me."

"That's a noble and tragic sentiment, Mary," Preuss said. "But not, I'm afraid, a terribly accurate one. There was someone else."

23

William Seldon surprised Preuss by answering the front door himself. His hair was neatly combed and he looked natty in a crisp polo shirt and pressed khakis with boat shoes and no socks. He looked every inch the wealthy suburban retiree. Somewhere in the house, Bandit was barking his head off.

"Come in, come in," he said to Preuss, and stepped aside from the doorway. He acted like he was expecting Preuss. But as Preuss walked past him, he noticed the blank look in Seldon's blue eyes, as though he weren't entirely present.

Seldon led him through to the dining room, which was set with two places for dinner.

"Sit down," Seldon said. "You're just in time."

Preuss sat on one of the side chairs. Seldon sat at the head of the table, with his hands clasped at his place in front of him as though awaiting his next set of instructions.

He stared hard at Preuss. "Have we met before?"

Before Preuss could respond, hard steps clattered over the wooden floors. Then he heard Christine Seldon's voice. "Honey, who was—"

She stopped when she saw him. "What are you doing here?"

Not at all pleased to see me, Preuss thought. Where's that big smile now? Where's that show-offy piano flourish?

"Your husband let me in," he said.

She threw a withering glance at Seldon. Who, for his part, didn't notice; he was staring straight ahead, like an automaton that had been shut down. Preuss could tell by the expression on her face that Christine was about to castigate William, but then thought better of it. Have to maintain a face for the company, even if the company is completely unwanted.

"I'm going to have to ask you to leave," she said.

"Not until I get some answers."

She considered that, and then said, "Why don't we go into the family room."

She held out a hand, inviting Preuss to leave the table. He followed her into the book-lined room where they had met before. William trailed after them, and sat beside his wife on the sofa. Preuss could hear the German Shepherd barking in another part of the house.

"Where is Bandit?" Seldon asked.

Instead of replying, Christine Seldon said, "Mr. Preuss, I wish my husband hadn't invited you in just now. We don't really have time to talk. We're just about to sit down to a late dinner, as you can see."

"This won't take long."

"Was there something you wanted?"

"Yes," he said. "The truth would be nice."

She crossed one knee over the other and clasped her hands around it. "I beg your pardon?" she said sweetly.

"That's what I came for. The truth."

"I'm afraid I don't know what you're talking about." She gave him a pained smile, as though deeply embarrassed for him.

He said, "I'm talking about what really happened when your husband's first wife was killed."

Preuss looked at Seldon. He hated to speak as though the man weren't in the room, but Seldon seemed elsewhere. He sat scowling, as though having a silent argument with himself.

"Is that different from the official version?" Christine asked. "Because this has all been adjudicated in the courts."

"It's not different," Preuss admitted. "But it does flesh out the official version."

She waited, saying nothing.

"For example, I think you and your husband had been seeing each other for a long time before you told me you met in New York. My first thought was that William here"—he pointed the top of his head at Seldon, who was still oblivious—"asked his elder son to find somebody to do a dirty job for him. Then Lawrence asked Mary to put him in touch with Mary's ex-boyfriend, Ray Douglas. Douglas was a tough, troubled kid in school and might have been the only guy Larry could think of who could handle what was supposed to happen."

"Which was?"

"Larry and your husband were supposed to convince Ray to get Claire out of your hair somehow before she reorganized the company. Then you and William could get married before the business went public."

Christine Seldon listened without a word, stone-faced.

"Afterward, Ray was supposed to leave and not come back. But the cops picked him up before he could get away."

"That's quite a story," Christine Seldon said.

"It's not over. Before Ray died in prison and told his daughter someone put him up to the kidnapping, I originally thought he was talking about William here."

"That's ridiculous," she said.

Seldon roused himself and looked around. "Where's Bandit?" he asked, as if just noticing the animal wasn't there.

Sitting beside him, Christine reached out and laid a hand on his arm. "Bill, please."

"No," Seldon said, growing agitated, "where's Bandit? I hear him. What have you done with Bandit?"

"Bandit's fine. He's just—"

Seldon tried to stand up, but Christine held his arm and pulled him back to the sofa. "Sit down, honey."

"I want my dog!"

"Sit down and keep quiet!"

Seldon calmed down immediately.

"Now just sit there and don't say anything," she said. "Until we clear up the trouble you started."

Seldon seemed to shrink back into himself. Then he looked up and saw Preuss sitting across from him. "Have we met?"

"Bill," Christine said, "be quiet."

"Of course, you're right," Preuss said to her. "That's not how it happened at all."

"I told you," Christine said. "My husband could never do something like that."

"That's true. As I discovered, he was incapable of it. Even back then, his Alzheimer's was too advanced. Twenty years ago, he wouldn't have been capable of organizing a series of events like the death of his first wife."

She sat back and smiled in triumph. "Then are you through? Because our dinner—"

"But you would."

"Excuse me?"

"Your husband was showing signs of Alzheimer's while he was still married to Claire. Claire knew that. And she also knew he was seeing you. You didn't even bother to hide it. In fact, you were just the latest in a long line of women he'd been with over the course of their marriage. She decided she'd had enough. She was going to change the structure of the company to cut him out.

"But his thought processes were failing by then," Preuss continued. "He not only couldn't run the company, he wouldn't have had the wherewithal to arrange for the murder of his wife. But you would. *You're* the one who asked Larry to find someone to take care of Claire. Maybe you didn't want her dead, maybe you just wanted her scared enough to get her out of the picture, or at the least drop her plan to reorganize. And Larry thought of Ray Douglas, and asked his sister to put him in touch with Ray. And to her everlasting regret since then, she did."

"Do you know how crazy that sounds?"

"It doesn't sound crazy to me at all, Christine. Not given the personalities involved."

"It's not even worth denying," she said.

Here Seldon picked his head up and inhaled deeply and let it all out, as though preparing for a race. "Yes," he said.

"William, please," she snapped.

But Preuss was by his side in an instant. "What do you want to say?"

"Yes," Seldon repeated. "That's what happened." He spoke calmly, and Christine stared at him as though she wanted to rip his tongue out through his throat.

"Quiet!" she shouted. She reached over to grab him, but Preuss blocked her hand.

"She told me," Seldon said. "She told me we had to get Claire out of the way. But I said no. I said no. We couldn't do that."

"You didn't say no, you fool," Christine hissed. "You thought it was a wonderful idea. But you don't remember, do you, with that Swiss cheese brain of yours, how you said it was a *wonderful* idea? But you couldn't bring yourself to get it started. So I had to do it. *I* made it happen."

"What did you promise Larry if he helped you? That you'd make Bill retire and give Larry charge of the company?"

"Of course. Under this one"—she made a dismissive toss of her head toward her husband—"things were going downhill. Larry was anxious to step in and save it."

"And that's why he got involved in a scheme against his own mother?"

"He didn't know that psycho was going to kill her. I told him I just wanted somebody to threaten her enough to make her change her plans for the business. But I told Ray Douglas to do whatever he had to do to get rid of her. He had some crazy idea about being the chief of police, so I convinced him killing Claire and then coming back to solve the crime would make that happen."

"You're the one who put Ray Douglas up to it."

"I told him when she'd be alone in the house. I gave him enough money to leave afterward."

"But he stopped to pick up his daughter at school before he left."

"That moron," she spat. "He would have gotten away and none of this would have come to light if he'd just left town the way he was supposed to."

But he couldn't, Preuss thought. He wouldn't leave without his little girl. Jessie Douglas was right when she said her father always loved her.

"Yes," William Seldon said.

"Bill, shut your mouth!"

Seldon pointed at his wife. "She talked with Ray. That's just what she did. I remember that."

"He doesn't know what he's talking about," Christine said. "He's so far gone he doesn't even remember what day it is."

"He sounds pretty sure to me," Preuss said.

"You'll never prove it," she said. "Who's going to testify? *This one?*" She pointed her chin at her husband. "Good luck with that."

"Oh," Preuss said, "I think we'll come up with something."

"Well, you'll never get a confession from me. And you have no other evidence. It'll be your word against mine."

"Not necessarily."

"What did you do," she sneered, "record this?"

"No," Preuss said. "But they did."

Preuss stood and pointed out the window into the back yard, where two men stood, flanked by a trio of uniformed officers.

"That handsome fellow on the left," Preuss said, "is Detective Reginald Trombley from the Ferndale Police Department. The one next to him is Detective Michael Luedke, from the Bloomfield Hills Police. He made the recording through my phone. He also has a warrant for your arrest."

"For what?"

"Aiding and abetting the murder of Claire Seldon, for starters."

On the other side of the picture window, Luedke held up a bundle of papers.

"There must be a statute of limitation," Christine said. "This happened almost twenty years ago."

"There's no statute of limitation on murder in Michigan. But there is a statute that says someone convicted of aiding and abetting will be sentenced for the principle offense. Which in this case is murder."

Trombley and the other detective knocked on the rear door. In another room of the house, Bandit was barking incessantly. William

Seldon tottered to his feet and, like the perfect host, went over to let the officers in.

Luedke went through the formalities.

"Wait," Christine said, as one of the uniformed officers started to lead her away. "Who's going to take care of my husband? He can't take care of himself—he's like an infant! Wait!"

"What's happening?" William Seldon said. Somewhere in the house, Bandit howled. "Christine? Christine! Where are you going?"

Christine struggled against Luedke's grip, but he guided her out to the scout car parked in the long driveway.

"Is she out there?" Preuss asked Trombley.

"In my car."

Trombley went back outside and returned with a tall woman with black hair worn short, almost shaved, except for the fashionable lock that swept down across the side of her face.

She stopped when she saw William Seldon standing in the middle of the room, looking scared and disoriented.

"Oh my god," she said softly. "Look at him."

"Who are you?" Seldon demanded.

Mary Seldon stepped forward. "Your daughter. Mary."

"I don't have a daughter!" he whined.

"Oh, yes you do," she said. She took his arm. "Sit down over here."

Still befuddled, Seldon struggled for a moment, then let her lead him.

Seated beside her, he looked at her closely. "Have we met?"

"We have," she said. She examined her father as intensively as he looked at her.

She turned to Preuss. "I never realized he was this bad."

"Do I know you?" Seldon asked her again.

"I'm your daughter. And you're going to have to answer for what you did."

"But what did I do?" He looked from his daughter to Preuss.

"He'll never stand trial," Preuss said. "He'll be institutionalized."

She acknowledged the truth of that with a nod.

"He's going to need someone to stay with him," Preuss said. "At least until things get sorted out."

"It'd be more than he ever did for me," Mary said.

Lost and confused, William Seldon looked tiny, almost like a child, sitting beside her. He began to rock back and forth.

"But the bastard is still my father," she murmured.

"Do you know where Bandit is?" he asked her in a small, frightened voice.

Preuss could tell she was sorting through all the different ways of answering that question.

She and Preuss exchanged a glance, and she seemed to come to some decision.

She patted her father's arm and said, "Don't worry. He's safe."

24

"Lawrence Seldon is in custody," Trombley said.

They stood outside the Seldon home, watching Christine Seldon being driven off in the back of a police cruiser.

"Good," said Preuss.

"I'm going back to the station to interview him before he transfers up to County," Trombley said. "I talk with one of the other guests at the party the night of the Douglas girl's death. Evidently Lawrence disappeared for an hour. Nobody knew what happened to him."

"Long enough to drive to Ferndale, try to persuade Jessie Douglas not to go any further, and kill her when she refused."

"We'll get a confession out of him. Even without it, there'll be enough to put him away."

"Let me know what he says," Preuss said. "It's pretty clear he killed Jessie Douglas to stop her from finding the answer to what her father told her. But I'm curious to know what his rationale was for helping his mother get killed."

"He might not have known that was going to happen."

"Yeah, that's what Mary tried to tell me."

"You don't believe it?"

Preuss shrugged. "What kind of son helps kill his mother?"

Trombley shook his head. "What a world."

"I'm betting he wanted control over the company so badly," Preuss said, "he'd do anything to get his mother and father out of the way. From what Mary told me, their father turned the boys against their mother, and treated them terribly. Larry probably thought control of the company was his recompense for it all."

Trombley rubbed his thumb and first two fingers together in the universal hand gesture for money. "Makes the world go round, my brother."

"That's a fact," said Martin Preuss.

He spent what was left of the evening with Toby. Preuss was never so happy to see his beloved son as he was in the chaotic aftermath of a case coming to closure.

Especially this one.

He held Toby sitting on the side of the boy's bed, feeling his warmth, inhaling his clean post-bath apple scent, talking about the resolution of the Douglas case. Two damaged men and one woman whose actions converged to change—and in some cases end—their families' lives.

And leaving their daughters' lives in tatters, a state that might now extend at least through the next generation, in the case of Jessie Douglas's little girl.

"I hope Renee Cacavelli learned enough about parenting to help Angie survive her childhood. At least in better shape than Jessie made it through the wreckage of hers. There'd be a smidgen of hope for her."

Breathing softly, regularly, Toby listened.

"As for Mary Seldon, I don't know what to tell you, Toby. Is she taking care of her father because she's had a change of heart toward him? Or because she wants to get close enough to take over the company, like her brother Larry? Or she wants to pay him back for what he did—or didn't do—to her?"

Toby offered his opinion in a series of sad hums and wise words only he could understand.

"I know, it's a mystery. And you get it, you old soul," Preuss said. He pulled Toby even closer. "You're way ahead me. As usual."

Toby leaned against his father's shoulder, and Preuss sat rocking his beautiful, vulnerable, eternally innocent child until the boy fell asleep.

Then Preuss stretched him out carefully on the bed and covered him with a sheet against the chill of the group home's air conditioning. He kissed his son goodnight, and made his way back to the dark, empty house in Ferndale.

Acknowledgements

My thanks to Jerry van Rossum for his suggestions and information about organizational structures. Thanks to the Royal Oak Public Library, where this book was mostly written. Appreciations to Genevieve Scholl for her editing, and to Rich Carnahan of Publish Pros for his design expertise.

Warmest thanks to my readers, whose support for this series is more gratifying than they can know.

As always, thanks to my wife Suzanne Allen for her love, support, and astute reading. Above all, my continuing grateful appreciation to Jamie Kril, the model for Toby, whose memory and loving spirit guide these pages.

Also by Donald Levin

CRIMES OF LOVE | BOOK 1

One cold November night, police detective Martin Preuss joins a frantic search for a seven-year-old girl with epilepsy who has disappeared from the streets of his suburban Detroit community. Unwilling to let go after the Oakland County Sheriff's Office takes the case from his city agency, he strikes out on his own, following leads across the entire metropolitan region. Probing deep into the anguished lives of all those who came into contact with the missing girl, Preuss must summon all his skills and resources to solve the many crimes of love he uncovers.

THE BAKER'S MEN | BOOK 2

Easter, 2009. The nation is still reeling from the previous year's financial crisis. Ferndale Police detective Martin Preuss is spending a quiet evening with his son Toby when he's called out to investigate a savage after-hours shooting at a bakery in his suburban Detroit community. Was it a random burglary gone wrong? A cold-blooded execution linked to Detroit's drug trade? Most frightening of all, is there a terrorist connection with the Iraqi War vets who work at the store? Struggling with these questions, frustrated by the dizzying uncertainties of the case and hindered by the treachery of his own colleagues who scheme against him Preuss is drawn into a whirlwind of greed, violence, and revenge that spans generations across metropolitan Detroit.

GUILT IN HIDING | BOOK 3

The third entry in the Martin Preuss mystery series finds Preuss called out to search for a van that has disappeared along with the woman who was driving and her passenger, a handicapped young man. Working through layer upon layer of secrets, Preuss exposes a multitude of contemporary crimes with roots in the twentieth century's darkest period. Complex, chilling, and compulsively readable, *Guilt in Hiding* finds Preuss investigating the most disturbing and unforgettable crimes of his career.

THE FORGOTTEN CHILD | BOOK 4

Newly retired Martin Preuss passes his days quietly with his beloved son Toby. When a friend asks him to look for a boy who disappeared forty years ago, the former investigator gradually becomes consumed with finding the forgotten child. Meanwhile, ex-colleague Janey Cahill persuades him to help her locate the missing father of a troubled young girl. Juggling both cases, Preuss revisits the countercultural fervor of Detroit in the 1970s-and plunges into hidden worlds of guilty secrets and dark crimes that won't stay buried.